Dave Zeltserman lives in the Boston area with his wife, Judy. He is a die-hard Patriots and Red Sox fan; and when he's not writing crime fiction he spends his time working on his black belt in Kung Fu. Serpent's Tail also publishes *Pariah* and *Small Crimes*.

Praise for *Pariah*

"*Pariah* is all I know of bliss and lament...bliss at reading a superb novel and lament at knowing that Dave Zeltserman has now raised the bar so high, we're screwed. This is the perfect pitch of reality, history crime, celebrity, plagiarism, and sheer astounding writing. It needs a whole new genre name... It's beyond mystery, literature, a socio/economic tract, a scathing insight into the nature of celebrity and in Kyle Nevin, we have the darkest, most alluring noir character ever to come down the South Boston Pike or anywhere else in literature either. I want more of Kyle and more of this superb shotgun blast of a narrative... If every writer has one great book in them, then Dave can rest easy, he has his and it's to our delight and deepest envy" Ken Bruen

"Mean like bad whiskey and sophisticated like good scotch, *Pariah* is a rare find and a scorching read. This accomplished novel features a great blend of strong narrative voice and a realistic, multi-layered plot that lays bare the dark soul of South Boston's underworld. In Kyle Nevin, his main character, Zeltserman has a dark Celine creation that is as literary as he is noir. To my mind this novel provides the final word on the Southie's demise and does so more artfully than its predecessors. Brimming with historical anecdote, rife with keen sociological insight, Zeltserman invests his novel with a veracity found mostly in non-fiction. However, this is a novel and a damn entertaining one, one that reminds us that reading the book truly is more informing and riveting than seeing the movie" Cortright McMeel

Small Crimes

"Zeltserman delves deeply into his specialty, an unorthodox look at the criminal mind – the 'unlucky' guy who can fool himself way too long. It kept me turning pages and glancing over my shoulder" Vicki Hendricks

"*Small Crimes* is a superbly crafted tale that takes the best from mid-century noir fiction and drops it expertly into the twenty-first century. Like the very best of modern noir, this is a story told in shades of grey. Immensely subtle, and written with a rare maturity and confidence, the story of troubled ex-con/ex-cop Joe Denton always keeps you guessing. This deserves to be massive. At the very least, it must surely be Dave Zeltserman's breakthrough novel" Allan Guthrie

"So noir…all the way to a surprisingly bold ending… Fairly zips along" *Guardian*

"Zeltserman creates an intense atmospheric maze for readers to observe Denton's twisting and turning between his rocks and hard places. Denton is one of the best-realised characters I have read in this genre, and the powerfully noirish, uncompromising plot, which truly keeps one guessing from page to page, culminates with a genuinely astonishing finale" *Sunday Express*

"Zeltserman's breakthrough crime novel deserves comparison with the best of James Ellroy" *Publishers Weekly*

Killer

——Dave Zeltserman——

A complete catalogue record for this book can be obtained from the
British Library on request

The right of Dave Zeltserman to be identified as the author of this work
has been asserted by him in accordance with the Copyright, Designs and
Patents Act 1988

First published in 2010 by Serpent's Tail,
an imprint of Profile Books Ltd
3A Exmouth House
Pine Street
London EC1R 0JH
website: www.serpentstail.com

ISBN 978 184668 644 3

Designed and typeset by folio at Neuadd Bwll, Llanwrtyd Wells

Printed in Great Britain by CPI Bookmarque,
Croydon, CR0 4TD

10 9 8 7 6 5 4 3 2 1

This book is printed on FSC certified paper

Mixed Sources
Product group from well-managed
forests and other controlled sources
www.fsc.org Cert no. TT-COC-002227
© 1996 Forest Stewardship Council
FSC

acknowledgements

There are a lot of people I would like to thank.

Once again, my beautiful wife, Judy, who has always been there for me.

To my editor, John Williams, and my publisher, Pete Ayrton, for all of their help and support, and mostly for believing in me. Without John and Pete, my 'man out of prison' trilogy would've ended with *Small Crimes*. It's because of them that I ended up writing *Pariah* and *Killer*.

To all my early readers and their great feedback: Laurie Pzena, Mike Lombardi, Jeff Michaels, and especially Alan Luedeking, who is my unofficial editor, providing me invaluable line edits before I ever show the book to anyone.

To my crack team at Serpent's Tail and Profile Books: Ruth Petrie, Emily Berry and Niamh Murray for their superb efforts in copy editing, proofing, and getting the book out there. Also to Jamie Keenan for creating one of the best book covers I've seen. And in advance to Rebecca Gray and Meryl Zegarek, who've both been tireless in their previous efforts in promoting *Small Crimes* and *Pariah*, and I'm sure will be doing an equally great job with *Killer*. I'd also like to thank David Kanell at Kingdom Books, Alex Green at Back Page Books, Patrick Millikin at Poisoned Pen Bookstore and David Thompson at Murder by the Book for all the support they've given me and my books in the past.

to ed gorman

chapter 1

1993

"What if I gave them Salvatore Lombard?"

That gets my lawyer's attention. It would have to, me offering up Boston's top crime boss. Up until that moment he'd only been going through the motions, halfheartedly suggesting that he might be able to cut me a deal for thirty years, but using a tone which indicated he didn't really believe that. I can't blame him. I've already seen the same videotapes and wire tap transcripts that he has. The state has me dead to rights for a long laundry list of crimes including extortion, a shitload of Mann Act violations and attempted murder. My busting up an undercover cop's skull with a crowbar was only icing on the cake as far as they were concerned.

"You're sure about this?" he asks.

I nod. This wasn't a spur of the moment decision on my part. It was something I'd been mulling over for weeks, ever since I realized someone in Lombard's organization must've given up the operation. This was the reason I fired the lawyer Lombard had cherry-picked for me, and had my wife, Jenny, find me a virgin one, someone not connected. I'm forty-eight, and maybe betraying Lombard means I'm never going to see forty-nine, but I'll be fucked if I'm going to be buried in a prison cell for the next thirty years.

"And you can tie him to all this?"

"Yeah."

"That might change things," he admits. "Let me see what I can do."

His face is flushed now. He stands up abruptly and knocks on the small square Plexiglas window embedded in the locked door, and two guards come into the room to escort me to my cell. Less than an hour later I'm brought back to the same room. My lawyer's waiting for me, his face still flushed, maybe even a bit shiny at this point. I take the chair opposite him, and we both wait patiently until the guards leave the room and close the door behind them.

"If you can really deliver Salvatore Lombard—"

"I can."

"Then I can get you fourteen years," he says. "This is a gift given what they have on you."

"I need better than that."

He stares at me, his eyes widening as if I'm crazy. "Leonard, let me try to impress on you how generous their offer is. I know the DA must be salivating over the prospect of nailing Lombard, but fourteen years is the best he can give you without inciting a riot within the police department after what you did to that officer, not to mention those other people. I wouldn't have a prayer of doing better than that if this went to trial—"

"I can do the fourteen years. That's not what I'm saying."

"Then what?"

I shift in my seat, my gaze wandering past him. "If I give up Lombard he'll tie me to other felonies. I need immunity from those. Fourteen years is all I do regardless of what else I confess to."

"What else did you do?"

I shake my head. "When we have a deal in place I'll give the rest to the DA."

My lawyer gives me a funny look, but he gets up again and signals through the Plexiglas window. The guards let him out, but this time they don't bother taking me back to my cell. I sit alone for no more than fifteen minutes before my lawyer is let back in. His eyes are hard on mine as he nods.

"As long as there's no crimes involving children, no child porn, and no sex crimes, the DA's willing to give you a free pass on everything else if what you give them can be verified and is enough for a conviction."

"We've got a deal then," I tell him.

My lawyer and I meet with the DA. After I'm given the paperwork for the deal my lawyer has worked out, I give the DA what he needs. It takes them three weeks to check it out, but once they have Lombard charged, we all meet again so I can outline the rest of my crimes, the ones I'm going to be given immunity for. It takes a while. There are so many of them. When I go over the twenty-eight murders that I did for Salvatore Lombard, the DA's face turns ashen. Involuntarily, my lawyer's lips twist into a sick smile, almost as if I'm pulling something over on him too.

I breathe easier after that. Ever since I fired Lombard's chosen lawyer, I was expecting Lombard to either find a way to kill me or to leak my involvement with those killings to make sure I couldn't cut any deal. I guess he couldn't figure out a way of doing either of them without screwing himself. Anyway, a hell of a weight off my chest…

chapter 2

present

Someone was moaning within the cell block. The noise was muffled; whoever it was must've had his face buried in the mattress. I sat and listened, trying to figure out which cell it was coming from and whether the moaning was the result of an inmate humping his mattress or sobbing into it. Not that I cared, but I'd been up several hours now and welcomed the distraction. The hours when I waited for the lights to be turned on were the hardest. Early on at Cedar Junction, when Jenny was putting the maximum she could into my prison commissary account, I had been able to buy myself a reading light and those hours weren't so bad. Once she came down with cancer, that changed, and it wasn't long before the only money coming in was from my work detail, which paid all of eight cents an hour. As much as I hated doing it I sold my reading light when my last bulb blew. I couldn't afford more bulbs; the little money I got was needed to buy necessities like soap and toilet paper. After that I was no longer able to escape from those quiet early hours alone with myself by reading.

If I were back in Cedar Junction, other inmates right now

would be giving this guy hell and letting him know in explicit detail what would be happening to his rectum the next day if he didn't shut the fuck up. Not here, though. Most of the inmates knew they were lucky to be held at a medium security prison. They knew there were far worse places they could be sent, places like Cedar Junction. And that they'd end up in one of those shitholes if they acted up.

There were no windows in the cell block, but still, there was never a true darkness here; only a murky grayness. The same had been true at Cedar Junction. At night both prisons kept a bank of fluorescent lights flickering on beyond the hallway. It was probably a prison regulation, at least in Massachusetts.

My internal clock told me it was five-thirty. At six o'clock every morning the lights are turned on and a horn is blasted solidly for a full minute to rudely awaken any of the lucky ones who had managed to sleep through the night. After the lights and the horn would come the showers, mess hall and then work details. Not for me, though, not with today being my last day in prison. A fourteen-year stretch done and finished with, and I'd be fucked if I was going to give anyone one last chance to ice me. Later that morning I had one last appointment with my "society reintegration" case worker, then I was done. Until then, I wasn't going to leave my cell for any other reason. Not that I believed anyone here had the intestinal fortitude to take me out, nor would it make any sense at this point for Lombard's boys to let it happen, but still, I'd feel like an idiot if I gave someone an opening at this late date.

The moaning had stopped. I had to turn my thoughts to something other than the stillness and quiet suffocating me, and I started thinking of Lombard's boys, of how surprised they had to be that I was going to be leaving here alive. I wondered briefly what odds were given on the street that I'd ever walk out of prison. Probably at least ten to one, and even then it would've been a sucker's bet. Not that Lombard's boys didn't make an effort. I knew they'd put a price on my head; at times I'd spot the ones who were gearing themselves up to make a go for it. But then I'd catch their eye, and I'd see their toughness fading fast, and I'd know they didn't have what it took to go through with it. The one time any of them tried it, there were three of them and they had set it up so that we'd be alone. When they made their move I moved faster and the one closest to me was on his knees vomiting blood, the other two quickly looking like scared school-children and scrambling to get away from me. After that, all the others that Lombard's boys tried to employ would make the same mistake of first trying to give me the hard stare in the eye, and then they'd be worthless.

That was all in the past. A different breed in prison now than what you can get on the outside. Things were soon going to get a lot easier for Lombard's boys, or harder, depending on how you looked at it.

I closed my eyes and listened for whether the moaning had started up again. It hadn't. Nothing but a dead, uneasy quiet. And far too much of it.

It was eleven o'clock when a guard dropped off the street clothes I had on at the time I was arrested all those years ago. I shed my prison dungarees and tee shirt, and put on my old clothes instead. My shoes, while dusty and scuffed, still fit. Nothing else did. My pants hung loosely on me, as did my shirt and leather jacket. I could've used a belt, but I guess they were holding that back until I was officially released. Still, it was good to be wearing my own clothes again. I was leaving the cell for the last time, and the only thing I took with me was a large envelope stuffed with papers. Nothing else was worth the bother.

While I was led through the cell block to the administrative wing of the prison, the guard escorting me made an offhand comment about this being my last day.

"Last hour, actually."

We walked in silence for a minute, then he muttered out of the side of his mouth, "No fucking justice."

I turned to give him a look. He was in his late twenties, about the same age as my youngest son. A big, awkward-looking kid with short blond hair, a pug nose and wide-set eyes. His flesh hung as loosely off him as my clothes did me, and it had the same color as boiled ham. There was something familiar about him, and I realized what it was. He looked enough like one of the guys I had taken out to be his son. I asked him what his name was and that startled him, alarm showing in his pink, fleshy face.

"For Chrissakes," I said, "I just want to know if you're related to Donald Sweet."

He shook his head.

"How about any of the other guys I, uh, had business with?"

Again, slowly, his head moved from side to side.

I looked him up and down, feeling a bit of my old self coming to the fore. "Shut the fuck up, then," I said. "And show some goddamned respect to your elders."

He stared straight ahead after that, his eyes glazed, his mouth having shrunk to a small, angry oval, and enough red seeping into his cheeks to make his flesh now more the color of a piece of bloodied ham. We walked in silence, and it wasn't until we arrived at my caseworker's office and I was halfway through the door that he remarked how maybe I didn't find justice in prison but that the streets knew how to take care of rats like me. I closed the door behind me, not bothering to turn around.

My caseworker, Theo Ogden, sat amongst the clutter of his small windowless office. He squinted at me from behind his thick glasses, and from the uneasy smile he gave it was clear he had overheard the guard's comment. "Mr March, I apologize for that," he said.

"I'll be hearing a lot worse soon," I said.

"Maybe so, but it was still uncalled for."

I shrugged it off, and took the chair across from his desk that he gestured for me to sit in. Theo was about the same age as the guard who brought me to him, but was much smaller both in height and weight, and the complete opposite in demeanor. Like the other times I'd met with him, he appeared disheveled and harried, and the suit he wore was about as big on him as my old clothes were on me.

After the way our last meeting went I wasn't expecting much, but the son of a gun surprised me by finding me a job cleaning a small office building in Waltham and renting me a furnished one-room apartment within walking distance of where I'd be working. The hours were going to be from 8 p.m. to 2 a.m., Monday through Saturday. I guess at that time the building would be empty except for security, and the building's tenants wouldn't ever see me, but still, I was amazed he was able to find anyone willing to hire me, even if it was only cleaning toilets and mopping floors. Theo had me starting my new job tonight, figuring I could use the money, and he stepped me through a budget he had drawn up – which showed how much I'd be taking in each month through public assistance and my job and what my expenses would be. It would be tight, with me hovering just above the poverty line, but it didn't much matter. If I ended up on the streets, it would still be better than where I'd spent the last fourteen years. And besides, I didn't expect to be around long enough to worry about it, not with my family history, and certainly not with Lombard's boys out there waiting, and maybe twenty-eight other families who might want to beat them to the punch.

Theo had finished walking me through the budget, and was now staring at me uneasily while he pulled at his lower lip. I knew he was deliberating whether to broach the same subject we had discussed the last few times we met. I saved him the trouble and told him I had no interest in leaving Massachusetts.

"Mr March, you should consider it," he said. "Even at this late date, I could arrange it if you let me."

"What would be the point? If someone wanted to find me bad enough, they'd track me down wherever I ran to."

"But you're making it so easy for them..." He stopped to take off his glasses and rub his eyes. With his glasses off he looked like a scrawny teenager who could've been president of his high school chess team instead of a prison caseworker who had to spend his days dealing with people like me. He put his glasses back on, ageing fifteen years in the process. His expression turning grave, he told me, "I'm not sure if you're aware of this, but the news has been running a lot of stories about you, and someone released a recent photo – one that was taken when you arrived here from Cedar Junction. People out there know what you look like, Mr March. I can't imagine it being too safe out there for you."

I handed him the envelope I had brought with me, the same one that was delivered two weeks ago filled with court documents outlining the five wrongful-death suits that had been brought against me, all filed by the same attorney. A perplexed frown took over Theo's features as he looked through the legal papers. Once it fully dawned on him what they meant, he looked up at me, blinking.

"There must be some way to work around this," he said.

"There isn't," I said. "And as you can see I need to be at

the Chelsea District Court in three weeks for the first of the lawsuits. They have to know I'm broke and that they're not going to collect any money. The lawyer's not doing this on a contingency basis, and he sure as fuck isn't doing it out of the goodness of his heart. Someone has to be paying the legal bills, either the families or, more likely, some other interested third party who arranged this. And probably for no other reason than to keep me from leaving the area."

Theo stared intently back at the paperwork, trying to figure out a way around the court appearances I was required to make. There wasn't any. I didn't have the money for the traveling back and forth if I were to move out of state, and even if I did it wouldn't have mattered. As soon as I was back in Chelsea for any of the court dates I'd be right in Lombard's backyard. Of course, I could've been making it sound more sinister than it really was. The lawsuits could've been filed for no other reason than to allow those families to have their day in court. But the expense of it made that seem unlikely. I took the papers from Theo's hands. It didn't much matter – if nothing else those lawsuits made it a quick argument between the two of us, because even if I could've I wasn't about to leave the Boston area. I wasn't sure why that was, at least nothing I could articulate, or really get a firm grip on. Of course I could've simply used the excuse that outside of my time in prison I'd lived my whole life around Boston and wasn't about to leave now, and that I was also hoping to re-establish contact with my kids. There was some truth to that, but there was something else, kind of a vague feeling that I needed to stay in the area. I just didn't know why exactly.

"I guess that's it," Theo said.

"Yeah, I guess it is."

"Maybe after these legal issues are settled you can think about relocation."

"Maybe," I agreed, although we both knew it wouldn't much matter by then. By that time, one way or another, it would be over. I'd be either dead or forgotten.

"We might as well finish processing you," Theo said with a tired smile.

He brought out a small stack of paperwork for me to sign, and while I did that he left the office. When he returned he had my personal effects – belt, wallet, watch and wedding ring. I was surprised no one had stolen the watch. It must've been tempting, especially with the thought of me dying in prison and no one ever finding out about it.

I slipped the belt on. It was too big for me, my pants still dragging down. I was going to have to carve out a few more holes in it. I almost asked Theo if he had a pocket knife, but he didn't seem the type and I had the thought that he'd panic and start thinking there were other reasons for me asking for one.

"Do you want me to arrange a taxi to take you to the commuter rail?" Theo asked after waiting for me to slip my wallet and wedding ring into my pants pocket. I did the same with my watch.

I shook my head. I had a hundred and seventy-two dollars on me, forty of which I had when I was arrested, the rest from my prison account and what Theo had been able to arrange as an advance on my monthly public assistance payments. I needed to conserve the little I had. The station was four and a half miles away. A taxi probably wouldn't cost more than a few bucks, but still, I'd walk it. The fresh air would do me good after all these years. Maybe it would help with my headache.

"Do the reporters know I'm being released today?"

Theo made a face. "They shouldn't. I've gotten a few calls, and have been practicing the art of misinformation by giving them Wednesday as your release date."

The door opened and a guard came in. He nodded at Theo,

then fixed his gaze past me, making sure to avoid eye contact. I stood up and thanked Theo for his decency.

Fortunately I didn't embarrass myself any further by gushing about how it was the only decency I'd been treated to over the past fourteen years, because I could clearly see the thoughts that passed through his eyes – that he was just doing his job and it wasn't his place to pass judgment on people, that he would leave that to God. He didn't say any of that. Instead he must've decided that discretion was the better part of valor. "Good luck to you, Mr March," he said. There was no hand offered, not that I expected one. I gathered up the paperwork he had given me, and left with the guard who was waiting to escort me out.

This guard was not the same one who had brought me to Theo's office. At least twenty years older, short-cropped gray hair, thick folds creasing his bulldog-shaped face. He didn't say a word to me while he led me to the front gate. I stepped outside, blinking, the sun big and bright overhead. The gate to the prison closed quietly behind me. There was no one out there waiting for me, no one in the prison had dropped a dime to the media about me being released today. I could understand that. I was an embarrassment to them. If they could've they would have thrown away the key and never let me out, but they didn't have that option. Not that there hadn't been guards trying to bait me over the years in the hope of extending my sentence, but it was always done half-heartedly, and always with some fear. They knew what I was capable of, and they had to be worried that I'd ignore the bait – which I always did – and get out someday. Now that they had to release me, they wanted it done as quietly as possible. I couldn't much blame them.

It was the middle of October, and it was cold out, maybe in the low forties, and with the wind whipping about, it felt colder. Within seconds I was feeling a chill deep in my bones. These days I got cold so damn easily. I zipped up my jacket and grabbed the open collar, trying to hold it closed as much as I could around the neck area. Then, after looking around to see if there were any cars idling nearby and seeing that there weren't, I set out on foot to catch a train.

chapter 3

1965

Word's out about Ernie Arlosi hitting a Trifecta at Suffolk Downs the other day, and we figure he should be happy to spread the wealth and kick some of his winnings over to us to keep him and his store in one piece. The dumb bastard ends up trying to put up a fight and I have to rap him a few times in the mouth with a piece of pipe while Steve and Joey smash up one of his freezers before he pays up. It was so fucking unnecessary, but some guys are just stupid that way. So we leave him with his mouth a bloody mess, and his store not much better. It all could've just gone down so easily, but he made his choice. Not that I care one way or the other.

The next day I'm by myself walking down Centennial Avenue when a silver Caddy rolls up next to me. Even before the window slides down I have a good idea whose car it is, and who's going to be sitting in the passenger seat. Sure enough it's Vincent DiGrassi. I don't recognize the muscle behind the wheel or the other wiseguy sitting in the backseat, but DiGrassi I recognize. Everyone knows he's Salvatore Lombard's right-hand man.

With his eyes DiGrassi motions for me to get in. I don't have a choice in the matter, but even if I did, I still would've gotten in there. The wiseguy in back gives me a cold stare as I join him. Neither DiGrassi nor the driver bother looking at me. The car takes off, driving straight down Centennial Avenue until it reaches Revere Beach Boulevard, then takes a right, goes through the rotary and on to Winthrop Parkway. The car keeps driving until it reaches a small battered-looking Colonial a few blocks from the ocean. We're on a dead-end street, no neighbors in sight, and close enough to one of the runways at Logan Airport where the noise of the planes taking off is deafening. We all get out of the car. As isolated as the place is, I doubt anybody sees us. The two wiseguys crowd me and hustle me into the house. DiGrassi tails behind.

They take me into the basement. Nobody's talking. The house shakes for a half a minute with the rumbling of a plane taking off. One of the wiseguys picks up a sword – the type a samurai might use – and unsheathes it. While he runs his thumb over the blade, he grins at me. It's a nasty grin, kind of like he's telling me how much he hopes he gets to hack me up with that sword. I don't pay him any attention. I don't pay any of them any attention.

DiGrassi speaks to me for the first time. He has a tenor's voice. Smooth, melodic, it makes me think of my pop's old records, the ones he used to play every Sunday. The voice doesn't fit DiGrassi's thick body and craggy, badly scarred face. He calls me punk, asks me how old I am. I tell him my name's Lenny March, not punk.

The wiseguy holding the sword hits me with its hilt in the stomach. I don't show any reaction to it. I think I surprise DiGrassi by not doubling over. At least, his right eyebrow arches for a second.

"I didn't ask you for your name, asshole," he says. "I know

your fucking name. Ernie Arlosi knows your fucking name. How old are you?"

"Twenty."

"How the fuck d'you get so shitbrained dumb in only twenty years?" he asks.

I can't help smiling. The words coming out of his mouth just don't match his high tenor's voice. The other wiseguy hits me in the mouth hard enough to loosen teeth. I taste blood, but I don't show any reaction other than that little smile of mine.

DiGrassi moves his face so it's inches from mine, so when he yells a spray of spit hits me. "You know who the fuck I am?"

"Yeah."

"You know who I work for?"

I nod.

"So how come you're so fucking stupid that you're going to beat up and rob a childhood friend of Mr Lombard's?"

I don't bother saying anything. I had no idea about it. I just thought Arlosi was some fat fuck in the neighborhood who shot his mouth off too much. DiGrassi moves his face an inch or too closer and roars at me that he wants to know who the other two fucks were who were with me. I stare back at him, still with the quarter-inch grin on my lips. I'm not going to tell him shit.

He backs away and his two thugs go to work. Every time they knock me down, I get back up on my feet. I don't show them shit. Nothing in my eyes, nothing in my expression. If this is the way it's going to end, so be it. Fuck them is all I can think.

A loud booming noise echoes in the basement. DiGrassi has pulled out a bigass gun and has blown a hole in the wall. His two thugs back away from me, and he fires three more shots into the same wall, then comes forward pressing the red-hot gun muzzle against my cheek, burning me. "I've had it with your bullshit," he yells, more spit flying into my face. "You give me those names now or I blow a fucking hole through your skull!"

I say nothing. I meet his stare, my own eyes dead. A snarl comes over his thick lips and he pulls the trigger.

Click.

The gun must've only had four bullets, and DiGrassi used them when he shot into the wall. He's grinning at me now, his two wiseguys laughing softly.

"The fucking balls on this," he tells his two wiseguys. "Not even a flinch." He looks me over, his grin growing wider. "Didn't piss his pants, and it don't smell like he crapped them either."

"A tough one," one of the wiseguys says.

DiGrassi nods, then tells me that my two buddies gave me up. "Each of them, less than five minutes, I swear to God. Don't worry, though, both those fuckers got worse beatings than you got."

So I realize what this is all about. An initiation, to see what I'm made of. And I passed. Still, I ask him what the fuck he wants with me, my voice not quite right given how swollen my mouth and jaw is, and how pissed I am at Steve and Joey. DiGrassi puts a meaty arm around my shoulder, looks at me with something close to respect.

"Kid, you did good," he says. "You showed real stones, and just as important, you ain't a rat. We can use someone like you. I want you to call me in a week after you've gotten a chance to clean up and get those bumps and bruises healed up, and we'll see if we can work something out."

He digs into his pocket and gives me a piece of paper with a phone number on it. I nod, put the paper away. He's appraising me, frowning slightly.

"March, what type of name is that?" he asks.

"My pop's family name was Marcusi. He changed it to March."

"Why the fuck'd he do that?"

I don't know the answer so I don't bother saying anything. DiGrassi's giving me a harder look, his frown growing deeper.

"You ain't full-blooded Italian, are you?" he asks.

I shake my head. "No, my mom's family came over from Germany."

"She at least Catholic?"

I again shake my head.

"Ah, fuck it," he says. "I wish you were full-blooded, but we can still use someone like you. Give me a call."

I tell him I will.

chapter 4

present

I took the commuter rail to South Station, and from there was going to have to catch a bus to Waltham. Nobody paid attention to me during the train ride, everyone locked into their own worlds. At least I could be thankful for that.

Once I got off at South Station I had an hour and a half to kill before my bus would be leaving, and I ended up walking down South Street to Beach Street, then on to Chinatown, figuring nobody would notice me there. First thing I did was buy some aspirin at a convenience store, hoping it would help with my headache. Next I found a hole-in-the-wall restaurant where for three dollars and fifty cents I had a plate of fried rice with pork and a pot of hot tea. Simply having ice in my water glass was a luxury that I'd forgotten about. I ate hunched over with my head bowed. There were only a handful of other people in the place. Anyone whose gaze wandered over to me would have only seen me as an old man wearing poorly fitting baggy clothes sitting alone at a cheap Chinatown restaurant.

When I was done eating, I took my fork with me to the men's room, stood in its lone stall and made several additional holes in my belt so I could use it to hold my pants up better. After that I paid my bill, left the restaurant, and made my way through Chinatown to Washington Street. I was surprised at how cleaned up the area had gotten with the X-rated theatres and most of the porn shops gone. There were still a couple of strip clubs, but they looked high end, and I watched as a small group of businessmen in suits walked into one of them. I continued on until I came to a jewelry store that advertised *Guaranteed Highest Prices Paid* in their window. The only person inside was a slug of a man who looked almost melted to the stool he sat perched on. He was in his fifties, not much hair, and had more bulges and chins than I'd seen on anyone in years. As I approached him he looked at me with mild disinterest. I handed him my Rolex watch and wedding ring, and he made a show of examining the Rolex with a jeweler's glass, then consulted a catalog even though he probably had the prices memorized.

"This genuine?" he asked, already knowing the answer.

"Yeah," I said. "It was given to me as a gift in 1980."

His earlier look of disinterest came back. "These Oyster quartz models, not a big demand. I might be able to give you three hundred…" He stopped as he caught the inscription on the back, *Deepest gratitude, Salvatore Lombard*. His eyes shot up at me and, as recognition hit him, the little color he had bled out, leaving his skin a sickly gray. "Eight hundred dollars," he coughed out, his voice breaking into a hoarse whisper with his mouth not quite working right, almost as if he had palsy. I asked him how much for my wedding ring. He weighed the ring on a scale and told me he could give me two hundred dollars for it.

More as a joke than anything else I asked if he could guarantee that that would be the highest price paid, and he seized up for a moment, making me think he was about to have a heart attack, before nodding fervently. I told him in that case to pay me the thousand bucks.

While he counted out the money for me, his stare remained frozen at his hands as if he were afraid of accidentally looking up and catching sight of me.

"You're the guy," he said.

I ignored him. So far he had counted out four hundred dollars in fifty-dollar bills, painstakingly making sure none of the bills were stuck together. When he reached seven hundred dollars he asked again about me being the guy, the one they've been talking about in the news who used to be a hit man.

"Just pay me what you owe me."

"Yeah, okay," he said, his tone hurt. "No reason to take that attitude." He hesitated for a few seconds, added, "But I know you're the guy."

"What the fuck difference does it make to you?"

He seemed stuck trying to come up with an answer to that. Once he had the stack of fifties laid out on the countertop in front of me, I picked it up, counted it myself and fattened up my wallet with it. A thousand bucks wasn't going to last long, but then again, I didn't expect to last long myself either. I was halfway out the shop when the jeweler finally thought of something to say and asked me how it felt. I gave him a puzzled look and he added, "You know what I'm asking. After killing all those people, and then cutting a deal by ratting Salvatore Lombard. So how does it feel? You have any remorse?"

Several of his chins had jutted out in a kind of forced bravado, but I could see the tentativeness in his liquid eyes. I wasn't even sure which he was asking me; whether I had remorse over being a rat or my murders. In any case, I didn't bother answering him. I walked out the store and let the wind slam the glass door shut.

By the time I returned back to South Station, a small line of tired-looking people were waiting to board the bus to Waltham. I got behind them, fitting right in. As far as I could tell nobody bothered to look at me, at least no more than casual, bored glances. If anybody recognized me, I couldn't tell. I took a seat in the last row. A discarded newspaper had been left on the floor. I picked it up and found a story about me starting on page five. It was a long article covering two pages. Fortunately it didn't include a picture of me, just one of the DA who had made the deal with me, and on the following page of the article, another picture showing several family members of one of the guys I had taken out.

Up until then I'd been avoiding as best I could all the stories about me, but I read this article carefully. My eyes had trouble focusing on the small print and the effort made my headache worse, but I did learn a few things. The DA had long since moved on to private practice, and he told the paper how making the deal he did with me still haunted him but that he had no way of knowing at that time about my involvement with Lombard. I had had no arrest record – not even as a juvenile – and was off the grid as far as the mob was concerned, and that up until my arrest for the business at the docks he had never heard of me, nor had anyone else in law enforcement. All that was probably true. It always amazed me with the shit I pulled as a kid that I was never arrested, and not only that, never even had any cops harassing me. Once I started working for Lombard, I was kept on the fringes, at least at first. Later when I started doing contracts for him we were careful to keep our association together quiet. For twenty-three years I was on the books at Jack's Discount Liquor Store on Lansing Street, and sometimes I actually spent my free hours uncrating boxes and stocking merchandise, although more often than not when I was there I would sit in the back room drinking scotch and studying the day's racing forms. Still, as invisible as I might have kept myself, it was carelessness on their part. The violence I committed at the docks should've alerted them to what I was, and then there was the inscription on the back of my Rolex. There was no excuse on their part for missing that, just as there was none on mine for wearing that Rolex out in public. Christ, I had gotten sloppy by then.

Of course, you can't always believe what you read in the papers. When I was first arrested, the papers and TV stations got half the shit wrong about what went down at the docks. Given that, I wasn't sure what to make of a claim the article made that the state had kept the details of my confession secret until six months ago. Maybe it was true. Quotes given in the article from several of the victims' families supported that. The other inmates at Cedar Junction, as well as the guards, knew what I'd done, but maybe that was just the word getting out from Lombard's organization. Maybe that knowledge was kept inside.

The explanation the state gave in that article for keeping the details of my confession secret was an outright lie – that it was part of the deal I made, and that it was only following a recent Superior Court decision that they were allowed to divulge my sealed confession. It was all bullshit. If my confession was sealed, that was done by them, not me. I guess they'd been hoping I'd never leave prison alive, and once they realized that I was going to they came up with this fairy tale to cover their asses. Thinking about it, I was amazed that these state officials were willing to keep the victims' families in the dark the way they did for so many years, but I guess it showed how afraid they were of the political fallout of having the public find out they cut a deal with a hit man with twenty-eight scalps tied to his belt.

The paper had talked to families of four of the guys I had taken out, and each of them were made to look like saints. I remembered these guys, and they were all dirty. I'm not saying they deserved to be killed, but they were far from the innocent choirboys they were made out to be. As I said before, you have to take what you read in the papers with a grain of salt. They get so much of the shit wrong.

By the time I finished with the article, my head was feeling like it was going to split apart. That wasn't that unusual for me. The last fourteen years I'd had headaches almost constantly, and had learned for the most part to ignore them. Sometimes they were worse than other times, and this time it was worse. Much worse. I fished out of my pocket the bottle of aspirin I'd bought earlier and chewed on a few tablets. When I looked up, a teenage boy sitting three rows up was twisted in his seat and staring fixated at me. His eyes slits, his face a hard plastic mask. There was no question that he recognized me. I stared back, and realized that it didn't make any fucking difference. I did what I did. People were going to know who I was, and sooner or later they were going to know where I was living. There was nothing I could do to change the past, and it was pointless thinking I could hide from it.

We kept up this staring contest, me and this boy, until a middle-aged woman who must've been this boy's mother realized that he was staring at me. She smiled apologetically at me, while at the same time reprimanding him. He shrugged her off and said something to her that I couldn't hear, but I knew from the panic in her face what it must've been. She grabbed him and forcibly moved him so that he was no longer looking at me. After that I stared out the window and watched while other cars rolled past us on the Mass Pike. If people inside the bus were staring at me, so be it. I had more important things to worry about. And more mundane things also.

Some of these more mundane things were necessities, like clothing. When Jenny was alive, I knew she was holding on to my old clothes for me, but once she died my kids probably threw it all out. Not that I knew for sure since Michael and Allison wouldn't take my calls and I had no idea how to reach

Paul, but that's most likely what happened. So all the clothes I had were what I was wearing. In retrospect, I should've packed up my prison jeans and tee shirts and underwear, but the thought of smelling that prison detergent a second longer seemed unbearable. Even more so, the prison stench I had grown to imagine soaked into that clothing. As it was I was going to have to spend a good deal of time scrubbing myself before I'd be able to get that stench off my skin. Of course, I had far more than the mundane to worry about, but at least for a little while that's what mercifully occupied my thoughts.

It didn't seem to take long before the bus came to a stop at a congested street corner and the driver announced that we were at the Moody Street stop. I pushed myself to my feet and stumbled off the bus, more tired than I would've thought. Bone weary could've described how I was feeling. While my work details kept me on my feet all day, I wasn't used to walking as much as I had today. I stood for a moment blinking as I looked around me. My first impression was that the area was a mix of yuppie and blue collar, with ethnic grocery stores and low-rent shops side by side with trendy-looking restaurants. I might've driven through Waltham once, I couldn't remember. I never had much to do with this area. Even though it was maybe ten miles west of Boston, this city could've been on the opposite side of the world as far as Revere and my old life were concerned.

I stood on the street corner thumbing through the papers Theo had given me, the cold from the wind numbing my face. When I found the apartment rental form, I squinted at it until my eyes adjusted enough for me to be able to read the address on it. Then I set off on foot.

The apartment Theo arranged for me was in the basement of a five-story brick tenement building which looked like it had been built in the sixties. When I first showed up there, the woman working in the office gave me an empty stare as if I were any other low-income elderly renter, and it was clear to me that she had no idea who I was. She was in her forties, heavy, with badly thinning red hair, and this dull look about her like she was someone who had little interest in anything, at least not enough to bother paying attention to what was in the news and in the papers. If she was the person Theo had dealt with, it explained why my application was accepted. Or maybe even if she knew that I was a confessed hit man, it still wouldn't have mattered to her.

Theo had set it up for the state to pay my security deposit and first month's rent as part of the DOC's prisoner reintegration program. After that I'd be responsible for all future payments, although I'd be getting additional state assistance checks for my first six months.

After I signed the required paperwork, the woman gave me a key and warned me that in a week I'd have to make my apartment available to their pest maintenance person; which meant clearing the countertops and storing any plates, glasses and silverware in boxes so the kitchen could be sprayed. I didn't bother telling her that that wasn't going to be a problem.

The apartment was a one-room studio with the kitchen and the living area all in the same space. It was supposed to be furnished, but there wasn't much in it. A small cot, about the same as what I'd slept on in prison, and a badly chipped dresser from the seventies whose three drawers all stuck. The kitchen area had a sink and enough counter space to maybe hold a few canisters and a toaster. Three cheaply built and falling apart cabinets were placed above a stove that was from the same era as the dresser, and an even older refrigerator sat wedged in the corner. The floor around the stove felt greasy, and the small amount of countertop also had a thin layer of grease and other dirt covering it. When I moved closer, I noticed the small pellets scattered about. Mouse droppings. A quick look showed the bathroom was in worse shape, and even dirtier. Not much more than a tiny cubbyhole that barely fit the toilet, sink and shower stall crammed into it.

The place had a dank, unhealthy smell to it. Given the old-style industrial tiles used in the flooring, it was clear that the basement had never been intended for habitation and must have been meant for storage and converted later to apartments. I knew from experience that the tiles were made with asbestos, and I noticed a few of them were crumbling which made them health hazards. It would probably cost a small fortune to dig them all out so they had chosen to ignore it. Later when I had time I'd buy some cheap carpeting to cover them and hope that that would save me from lung cancer. Yeah, I know, wishful thinking.

I stood still for a moment, taking in what five hundred and sixty dollars a month bought these days. A dirty, musty, pest-infested space of maybe four hundred square feet, which made it both spacious and luxurious compared to where I was coming from. I'd make do. First thing I'd have to do was clean the place and get a few items – a lamp, a radio, and a card table and folding chair so I'd have someplace to eat. That would have to be later, though. It was three o'clock and I had to report at eight for work, and the bone weariness I'd been feeling earlier was now more as if my bone marrow had been replaced with lead. Christ, I couldn't remember being this worn out. I moved over to the cot. The mattress had a brownish-yellowish stain running over it. I flipped it over and the other side wasn't much better. Fuck it. I took off my jacket and lay on my back on the mattress. The damn thing smelled heavily of perspiration and body odor, maybe even worse than what I'd had in prison, but I was out within seconds.

chapter 5

1969

I know he's dead. I think it happened when I cracked his head against the door. It wasn't that hard a blow, but he must've had something already wrong with him. Shit, this wasn't supposed to happen. I sneak a quick peek over at Charlie and Hank. They haven't caught on yet, so I keep up the act pretending the fucker's still breathing. This was only supposed to be a shakedown, and I don't want to let on yet that I've fucked up. My first kill, and it's a damn accident.

"You miserable cocksucking prick," I say, lifting the dead fucker by his collar, his head lolling limply to the side, "where the fuck's our money?" While holding him up with my left hand, I start hitting his dead face with my right fist.

Hank and Charlie are swapping jokes. They stop. The only sound is me punching that dead face. It doesn't sound much different than if I'd been pounding a cold slab of beef. Charlie tells me to relax, that there's no reason to work up such a sweat. I sense Hank moving closer so he can get a better look.

"Shit, Lenny, I think he's dead," Hank says.

"Fucker's just playing possum," I say. I'm breathing hard now from my exertion. I reach back to throw one last punch, but Hank grabs my arm and stops me.

"He's not playing. He's dead."

I make a face as if I still don't believe it. "In that case, I better fucking make sure, huh?" I pull my arm free from Hank's grip, grab a lead sap that I keep under my waistband, and hit the dead man hard enough in the skull to leave a three inch dent. I let go of the body and it drops with a thud to the floor.

"Fucking vicious sonofabitch," Charlie says, but he's laughing softly, maybe even with a little admiration. The two of them are taking it better than I would've thought.

Because it was only supposed to be a shakedown, none of us bothered wearing gloves. Hank and Charlie have been in the game longer than me, and they start walking around the room wiping off fingerprints. I bend down over the dead man, wipe my sap clean using his shirt, and pull out his wallet. There's three hundred dollars in it. He was on the books for five grand, but at least this is something. I tell Hank and Charlie about the money. "I knew the cocksucker was holding out on us," I say. I kick the body a couple of times in the chest, hard enough to have killed him if he wasn't already dead. I'd rather have Hank and Charlie think I'm a psycho then give them any hint about me worrying how Vincent DiGrassi is going to take this. And I am worried.

Hank and Charlie have worked their way to a back entrance. Hank tilts his head to one side, signaling for me to join them. I kick the dead body once last time and, as nonchalantly as I can, leave with them.

We walk quickly down an alley, then once we're a block away, at a more normal pace to a side street where we left the car. It's late, the streets are empty. Charlie's laughing softly, puts an arm around my shoulder and comments how I've got antifreeze running in my veins. Hank looks deep in thought. After Charlie pulls away, Hank moves close to me and tells me softly enough so only I can hear that DiGrassi isn't going to be happy. As if he's telling me something I don't know.

We still have some time before last call. I'm driving so I stop off at the Broken Drum. Since I'm the one who fucked up, I buy us each a half a dozen rounds, beating last call by minutes. The bartender's not happy pouring out so many rounds that late knowing how much longer he's going to have to keep the bar open, but he knows who we work for so he doesn't say anything. While we're drinking I notice for the first time how swollen and cut up my knuckles are. None of us talk much, it's almost as if we're at a wake. It's not as if the fucker didn't deserve a beating, but I don't think he's what any of us are thinking about – at least he's not who I'm thinking about. When we're done with our drinks, I drive Charlie and Hank back to Revere where we hooked up earlier, then I drive across the bridge to Chelsea and to my apartment.

It's not until three days later that I meet with Vincent DiGrassi again. It's in the backroom of a club in Revere. I feel some relief over where we're meeting. If he'd been planning to make an example of me and have me taken out in a bag, we would've been meeting someplace else, someplace more private, like that house in Winthrop where I'd had my initiation.

When I walk into the backroom, DiGrassi's waiting alone, which is another good sign. He gives me the evil eye and keeps it fixed on me while I take a chair across from him.

"You fucked up," he accuses me, his tenor's voice shaking with anger. "'Cause of you I got a dead business partner and five grand pissed out the window. What the fuck you have to say about that?"

I took the three hundred dollars that I had gotten off the corpse and toss it on the table. "You're better off without him," I say. "And this three hundred dollars is more than you were ever going to get willingly from that cocksucker. The other forty-seven hundred I'll make up on my end, which won't be all that hard once the other deadbeats out there hear about this."

I meet his stare. After a minute or so of this, there's a shift in his expression. A cautiousness. A consideration. He wets his lips, leans back in his chair. "You get off on beating this guy to death?" he asks.

"Hank and Charlie tell you that?"

"They just told me what happened."

I smile one of my rare smiles. "I didn't get off on it," I say. "I knew the guy was dead before they did. Everything I did afterwards was for their benefit."

DiGrassi's staring at me intently, maybe even a little concern showing in his eyes. "So how do you feel now?" he asks. "Anything bothering you?"

"I'm fine," I say. "I was just doing my job."

Again, with that intense stare as if he's trying to look into my soul. "You sleeping okay?" he asks.

"No different than usual. Eating okay, too."

"So this doesn't bother you at all?"

I shake my head. "Other than I got to kick in forty-seven hundred to make good, no."

"Nothing troubling your conscience?"

"What fucking conscience is this supposed to be?"

He's considering this. His eyes darken, almost as if a veil has lowered over them. "You're right, Lenny," he says at last. "The guy was a cheap sonofabitch chiseler, and fuck him now that he's worm food. Forget that forty-seven hundred also. Go out of town for a few weeks, make it a vacation. When you come back, we'll be changing how we use you."

I stand up and start towards the door. I have a good idea how he's going to be using me. At some subconscious level, maybe I'd known all along. I'd spent four years on the fringes for DiGrassi doing collections and other diddly shit, so maybe in a way I was auditioning, trying to show them I was more important than how they were wasting me. It had to've been something like that 'cause it made no sense for me to have accidentally killed the guy. I'm not that careless. Before leaving, I nod to DiGrassi.

chapter 6

present

The room was dark when I woke up. I lay blinking for a few seconds, disoriented, then I remembered where I was and how I had to be at work at eight o'clock. I thought about the list I had made earlier of what I needed to buy, and mentally added an alarm clock to it.

I pushed myself off the bed, my body stiff and an awful taste in my mouth. That taste must've come from the mattress; at some point I must've rolled off my back and had my face pressed against the damn thing. It took a moment or two to straighten my back, then I hobbled in the direction of the bathroom – or at least where I thought it was. I wanted to splash some water on my face and rinse my mouth to get that taste out of it. My eyes still hadn't adjusted to the darkness and my sense of bearing was all off and it took me several minutes of fumbling around the apartment walls before I found the bathroom door. The light switch for the bathroom was on the wall inside the door. I flipped it, turning on what must've been a thirty-watt bulb that had been left in the fixture above the sink. It barely lit the small closet-sized room.

There were no mirrors in the prisons I had been in for obvious reasons – you don't want inmates getting their hands on broken glass. The last ten years or so I avoided looking at anything where I could've caught a reflection of myself, so it was a shock when I looked in the small, cracked mirror above the sink. The dim light provided by the single bulb kept my face mostly buried in shadows, which probably added even more years to my appearance. Logically I knew I had aged a lot over my time in prison, but still, I wasn't expecting that old man staring back at me. My face had gotten so much thinner, narrower, and my ears and nose so much bigger and looking like something carved out of wood. I'd had my head shaved several months back by the prison barber, and my hair was now growing back white, not even gray. Of everything, though, it was my eyes and cheeks that seemed the most foreign to me – my cheeks hollowed out like those of a corpse, and my eyes sunk deep into the flesh. Fuck, I looked at least fifteen years older than I should've, and so much frailer than I imagined myself. I forced myself to look away, and cupped my hand under the faucet so I could rinse out my mouth. The water had a rusty, sour taste, and it didn't help at all. I splashed some of it on my face which didn't make me feel any cleaner. Since that was the only working light in the apartment, when I left the bathroom I kept the door open and the light on so I'd have some light in the room. I brought my papers back to the bathroom and squinted hard at each one until I found the form that had my work address, then grabbed my jacket and left the apartment.

It had gotten colder since I'd been out earlier. I found myself shivering as I made my way up several side streets to Moody Street. Once I reached Moody Street, I passed a coffee shop with a clock out front. It was twenty to eight; at least I'd woken up early enough that I'd be able to get to my job on time. I stopped in the coffee shop, bought a few jelly-filled doughnuts and a large coffee, and got directions for the street where I was going to be working. The young Hispanic girl working behind the cash register had a bright, infectious smile, and told me it shouldn't take more than ten minutes to get there. She was being too polite and cheerful to have recognized me, but I still dropped thirty cents change into her tip jar.

While I walked, I ate my doughnuts and drank my coffee, and no more than ten minutes later, as the girl had promised me, I approached a small three-story brick office building where I was supposed to report to work.

Inside I could see a lone security guard sitting at a desk. I walked up to the glass door and knocked on it. He looked up and gave me an empty stare before pushing himself to his feet and walking slowly to the door so he could get a better look at me. He was no older than thirty. A big awkward-looking kid with a buzz cut and a large round face that made his small dark eyes appear even smaller. He knew who I was. I could tell from how much trouble he was having making eye contact with me. Still, he pretended he didn't and asked through the intercom who I was and why I was there. I told him and he opened the door for me, mumbling that I should take a seat while he called for the building manager.

I sat in one of the two chairs in the lobby while he got on the phone. Less than a minute later a man about my height but much thicker in the trunk came out of the elevator to meet me. He was in his fifties, hard-looking, with ash-gray hair and a face that showed he had spent time in the ring when he was younger. He carried a clipboard in his left hand, and didn't bother introducing himself or offering his free hand. Instead he told me I was late, that I was supposed to be there at seven-thirty.

"I was told eight."

He stared at the clipboard before glancing back at me for as much as two seconds, his eyes darting back to his clipboard. "First day you're supposed to be here at seven-thirty," he said, repeating himself. "According to this, you know how to clean bathrooms, empty trash cans, and use a vacuum cleaner. That true?"

In my old days I would've answered him differently than I did, but those days were done with and whoever I was back then had been replaced by an old man. I told him it was true.

"Here's the deal," he said, his eyes fixed on his clipboard, almost as if he were afraid of catching another glimpse of me. "First three months you're on probation. You miss work, you're late or don't do a good enough job, you'll be fired, no notice, no nothing. Understand?"

"Yeah."

He nodded, more to himself than to me. "I got paperwork for you to fill out. Afterwards I'll show you where the supplies are kept and what you need to do. Okay?"

"Sure." I hesitated for a moment, then asked him if he knew who I was. That caught him by surprise. He nodded, muttered uncomfortably that he did.

"Then why d'you hire me?"

Again, he was caught off guard. He showed a befuddled look while stumbling about for a moment, then asked me if I was planning to kill any more people.

"No."

"Then if you can do the job, why shouldn't I hire you?" He seemed relieved to have come up with that answer and he looked at me for a brief second, a thin smile having cracked his face. "I live by the rule that people deserve a second chance," he muttered under his breath as if he were embarrassed by expressing these sentiments. With that, he turned from me expecting me to follow him, which I did. Instead of using the elevator, this time he took the stairs. I guess he figured he didn't want to be confined in a small elevator with me.

After filling out the paperwork that he gave me, I followed him on a quick ten-minute tour of the building where he showed me the supply closet, the dumpster out behind the building, and each of the nine offices I'd be cleaning, as well as the shared bathrooms on each floor. At no time did he bother offering me his name, nor did I bother asking him for it. He seemed too uncomfortable with me for me to engage him in any conversation, and was clearly trying to rush things along and be done with an especially unpleasant task. When he was finished with the tour he told me that the tenants were usually out of their offices by six each evening so there was little chance I'd run into any of them.

"If they're still working when you show up, skip their office and try again later," he added gruffly. He handed me a set of keys, each one marked to indicate which door it was for. "When you're done each night, check the keys in with the night guard. When you report to work pick up the keys from him also."

He hesitated for a moment before telling me that he usually left by seven each night so I probably wouldn't be seeing him again, at least not unless he needed to fire me. His stare drifted past me, as if he were looking for an escape route. He asked if I had any additional questions in a way which indicated that he hoped I didn't, so I told him I didn't, and he wasted no time in leaving. I gave him a head start so it wouldn't look like I was following him, then I headed back to the first floor and the supply closet located there.

I took the cart out and loaded it with a bucket, mop and cleaners, figuring I'd do the bathrooms first while I still had the energy for it. I had a second wind after conking out earlier, but there was no telling how long that would last, especially given all the recent changes in the routine that I'd settled into over the last fourteen years.

I worked methodically; first cleaning the sinks, then toilets, then mopping the floors. While I did this I couldn't help noticing how quiet it was. In prison I'd kept to myself and seldom talked with anyone, but there was always a buzz around me, always other inmates nearby, and I always had to be conscious of the threat that they posed. In a way that was good – it kept my mind occupied. It was only during those early morning hours when I'd be stuck alone with my thoughts. Early on when I had my reading light I could escape those hours with books, and later after I had to sell my light there'd still be enough noises coming from the cellblock to distract me – an inmate crying out in his sleep, threats being made, other sounds caused by God knows what. This was different. The only two people in the building were me and the kid playing security guard by the front door. The only noise breaking the quiet was what I made while I worked. I was going to have to buy a radio or portable compact disc player or something, because otherwise I didn't think I'd be able to bear the quiet.

I needed to distract myself from the memories that were pushing through the silence, and I forced myself instead to think of my pop, to remember what he was like and how he would react if he were alive now to see me cleaning bathrooms. It had been a long time since I'd thought of him, but I knew he'd be happy to see me at a real job and I knew what he'd tell me: "Nothing wrong with an honest day's work, son."

My pop was only forty-three when he died of a heart attack. I was fifteen at the time. From what I could remember he was a gentle, soft-spoken man, and later my mom and others would tell me how he'd worked hard every day of his life. Honest work, too. Him and my Uncle Lou built houses all up and down Blue Hill Avenue. Neither of them ever made much money from it, several times getting ripped off enough by contractors to keep them buried in a financial hole, but I couldn't remember either of them ever complaining about it. My Uncle Lou died young also. I think he was only forty-six when he bought it, and it was only a couple of years after my pop. Something about his lungs.

The last couple of years of my pop's life there would be such an overwhelming sadness in his eyes when he'd look at me. By the time I was thirteen I was all he and my mom had left with my brother Tony being killed in Vietnam and my brother Jim dying only a few months afterwards in a stupid accident during a summer job – being pushed out a window while moving furniture. I knew I was a disappointment to him with the little interest I showed in school and all the fights I kept getting into and the petty thefts and other little crimes. As far as the fights went, what the fuck did he expect? We were living in a blue-collar Catholic neighborhood, and my mom was Jewish, which as far as the other neighborhood kids were concerned meant I was Jewish, even if I was going to church every Sunday. Ever since I was five I was having kids lining up to challenge me to fights, claiming that I killed our Lord. I wasn't going to take that shit.

I don't know how Tony and Jim ignored that crap when they were kids, but I sure as fuck wasn't going to. Although I was small for my age, I was ruthless when I fought and went at it like a tornado being released. By the time I was fourteen I had enough strength where I could do some serious damage, as Tommy McClaughlin found out. It was brutal what I did to him – knocked unconscious, his jaw, cheekbones and skull all fractured, his face not much better than raw hamburger meat. I almost went into the juvenile system for that, probably would've except Tommy McClaughlin's old man refused to press charges. He wanted his kid to be able to have another go at me when he recovered. After all, it was embarrassing for him with his kid forty pounds heavier than me, and me being practically a Jew. We never did have that rematch. When Tommy healed up, he kept away from me. He knew what I was capable of, as did the other kids in the neighborhood. The last few months my pop was still alive I rarely got into fights, and when I did it was only with kids outside the neighborhood who didn't know any better, and none of them ever fared much better than Tommy did. By this time I was more careful to make sure there weren't any witnesses. I didn't want to see that horror in my pop's eyes again like I did that time when he was brought to the police station after Tommy.

I remember it was a week before he died when my pop took me out to dinner alone at a fancy steak house. He wanted to have a heart-to-heart with me, to impress on me the importance of an education and living a clean, honest life. I never much saw the point of being a wise ass, and tried to act as if I was buying what he was telling me. Maybe I convinced him, but more likely he knew it was going in one ear and out the other. After all, he and my Uncle Lou turned out to be examples of what you got from that type of hard work and honest lifestyle – you were taken advantage of your whole life and then you dropped dead before fifty. And it wasn't just them – my pop's father also died young, as did all my pop's uncles. I don't think any of them made it into their fifties, but they all worked hard each day of their life as laborers up until the moment they died. Fuck, my brothers who followed the rules and tried to live cleanly didn't even make it into their twenties.

In a lot of ways it didn't make sense for me to give up Salvatore Lombard. With my family history I never expected to make it to forty-eight let alone sixty-two, so why make that deal?

I spent a lot of time thinking about it in prison. For years I tried to convince myself that I did it as payback for whoever it was inside of Lombard's organization who gave me up to the Feds, especially since I had wanted to retire from that life and I'd let Lombard strong-arm me into running that business at the docks. Over time I realized that wasn't the reason, as much as I wanted it to be. What was mostly behind my making that deal was that I needed a glimmer of hope, no matter how dim, of someday walking out of prison. I don't think I could've managed inside without that. But that probably wasn't the only reason; at that point in my life I needed to come clean with what I'd done. I don't know, but I think that was behind what I did, at least at a subconscious level. But no matter how much I struggled over it, I could never be quite sure how much of a role that played in it, if any at all.

I had finished both bathrooms on the first floor and was pushing the cart towards the elevator when I realized I was mumbling under my breath, carrying on a one-sided conversation with my pop. Yeah, I was going to need a radio or something, otherwise this quiet would drive me nuts. Looking around sheepishly, I checked to see if the security guard was nearby and whether he could've overheard me. I didn't see him, and I pushed the cart past the elevator until I spotted him sitting behind the same security desk he'd been at earlier. I doubt he had heard me, he seemed too engrossed in the paperback he was reading. When I started to push the cart back to the elevator, he looked up, startled, as if I had spooked him. Our eyes met for a brief moment before he glanced back towards his paperback, his round pink face turning flaccid. If it wasn't clear enough earlier, it was clear then that the two of us were never going to have much of a conversation together while I worked there – he was terrified of me, and that wasn't going to change.

I pushed the cleaning cart into the elevator and took it to the second floor and started on the bathrooms there. Once I was done with those I moved up to the third floor, and then after those were done, started emptying trash cans throughout the building, then vacuuming each office and the hallways.

I was finished by one o'clock. I had no better place to be, and besides, I was supposed to be working until two so I stayed holed up in the last office I had vacuumed. They had a plush leather sofa in their lobby that was a hell of a lot more comfortable than the cot I had waiting for me. A few times I almost drifted off, my eyelids heavy, but I stayed awake until two, and then trotted back to the front security desk and checked the keys in with the apple-cheeked youth working there. He didn't say a word to me, nor me to him, and I knew that was the routine we had settled into, not that I should've expected much else.

Stepping outside I held my jacket collar tight against my throat, trying to seal off the cold. A wind was whipping about and I lowered my head against it. After half a block, I looked up, thinking that I had seen something out of the corner of my eye – a black sedan driving away with its headlights off. I must've imagined it because when I looked up the street was empty and the only noise I could hear was the wind. I stood staring bleary-eyed for a moment, then lowered my head again and quickened my pace.

chapter 7

1970

Carl Slagg's a big fucker. Large ruddy face, barrel-chested, and a good sixty pounds heavier and a half-foot taller than I am. The two of us are in a dive in Charlestown, a walk-down bar off of Washington Street. It's Saturday night and the place is packed with local toughs, sailors on leave, and chicks looking to drink free and maybe hook up for the night. I'm hoping Slagg doesn't pick any of these girls up, but with the way he's flashing his roll there's a good chance of it, especially given how shitfaced he is. There are some tough broads in the crowd, and I'm sure a few of them have already given some thought to trying to take that roll off him. It would be unfortunate if that happens. This is my first official hit for DiGrassi and I'm hoping it goes down easy. If Slagg leaves with one of these girls I'll have to take both of them out.

Slagg doesn't know me, and the few times he's glanced in my direction it's been with alcohol-glazed eyes that weren't paying much attention to anything. Word is that he ripped off a high-stakes poker game in Southie last Wednesday, walking away with twenty grand. Now he's celebrating. I followed him into this dive three hours ago, almost took him out during one of his trips to the bathroom to return the Irish whiskey he's been pouring down his throat, but I was told to take care of him outside the bar, so I'm waiting for him to leave.

DiGrassi didn't tell me the reason for taking Slagg out, nor was I going to ask him, but it wasn't too hard to figure out. I'd heard one of Lombard's boys was in the poker game that got ripped off, that the next day Lombard sent one of his men to let Slagg know there was a contract on his head but for half the money taken from the game – ten grand – he could fix the contract and see that it went away. Slagg, the dumb fuck, had to tell the guy to go fuck himself.

Slagg is one boisterous son of a bitch. He's slamming down shot after shot, all the while his voice booming through the bar as he argues Red Sox, Celtics and Bruins with anyone who'll listen to him. Now it's how without Bobby Orr the Bruins would still have won the Stanley Cup. Christ, the guy keeps proving over and over again that he's too dumb to live.

His voice dies away. He wipes a thick hand across his mouth, his eyes intent on a blonde dye-job standing near him, and she's eyeing him back. I'm sure she noticed his roll earlier.

He approaches her. His neck bends so his mouth is against her ear. She's buying what he's selling her, and I'm thinking how I'm going to be leaving two bodies later, but then Slagg goes too far. Whatever he tells her, it leaves her eyes like hard stones and her mouth showing hurt. He tries to physically move her from her barstool, but then a group of sailors standing nearby come to her rescue. It's four against one and I'm waiting for the first punch to be thrown, but Slagg's too fucking drunk and loses his train of thought and ends up stumbling away. He stops for a moment, then continues until he's heading up the stairs and out of the bar. I leave through a back door, moving fast to catch up with him.

He makes things easy for me, the dumb fuck. After walking half a block, he turns down an alley. Sure enough he's swaying a bit on his feet while he takes a leak in the alleyway. Watching him, it's like he's on a boat that's listing badly from side to side.

I have a .38 snub nose, but I see no reason to use it. Instead I take out a nine-inch stiletto blade and I have it in and out of his back before he ever realizes I'm behind him. He totters for a moment, then falls to his knees and pitches forwards, his face smacking against the brick wall before landing in the puddle he made. I know he's dead, I know I pierced his heart. I bend over anyway to check, and while I'm checking I also take the roll out of his pocket. Sixty-three hundred bucks. A nice bonus for the night, although I'm going to have to cough a good part of it up to Vincent DiGrassi.

It's three days later when I meet up with DiGrassi. We're being careful at this point to keep my connection with him and Lombard hidden. For six months I've been on the books at a liquor store over on Lansing Street so it looks like I'm gainfully employed. DiGrassi eyes me carefully. He knows things went smoothly with the hit. No witnesses, no fuss, no problems. What he wants to know is how I'm taking the killing and he's looking hard into my eyes to figure it out. There's nothing in there for him to see. He asks me anyway how I'm feeling and I tell him I'm sleeping as well as ever and eating even better. He grunts, satisfied, and as he gets up I hand him an envelope. Inside is three grand. He arches an eyebrow, and I tell him it's from the sixty-three hundred I took off Slagg. For a second I can see the calculating look in his eyes as he figures I should be handing over more than three grand – after all I'm being paid well for the hit, but the look fades and instead he nods and tells me he'll be in touch when needed.

My first official hit. As smooth as silk. And an extra thirty-three hundred to boot. Overall I'm feeling pretty good.

chapter 8

present

I had a restless night of it where I slept at most in five-minute stretches. I think the combination of the dank mustiness of the room and the smell of the mattress kept waking me. By morning I was tired but also alert with little chance of getting any more sleep. My back was stiffer than usual, and it took a while to maneuver myself off the bed, and then to simply straighten myself to the point where I could stand normally. I decided then I was going to buy a new bed. I wasn't going to be left with much once I bought the things I needed.

Without a blanket or sheets it had been too cold that night to sleep in my underwear so I'd worn my clothes to bed, and later ended up putting my jacket on. Now they felt gamey and oily on me, but they were all I had so I had to wear them again. In the morning light my apartment was even more of an eyesore – the walls cracked and stained, the plaster ceiling yellowed and crumbling in spots, the floors filthy. I stumbled to the bathroom to splash water on my face, this time being careful not to catch a glimpse of myself in the mirror. I wasn't up to that, not in the brighter light. Out of the corner of my eye I caught something scurrying towards the kitchen area, probably a mouse. I didn't bother looking for it, though. As soon as I was done in the bathroom I left the apartment.

It wasn't as cold as the day before with the sun out and the skies mostly clear, but still, I was shivering. I made my way back to Moody Street. The area was quiet with little traffic on the road and outside of myself, no one else on the sidewalks.

A clock outside a bar showed it was only ten past six. I walked a few blocks, first one side of the street, then the other, and found several greasy-spoon diners advertising breakfast, but the earliest any of them opened was six-thirty. I stepped into a twenty-four-hour convenience store and bought a large black coffee, and while I drank it I picked up a newspaper. I was on page one. The story had broken that I had been released from prison and somehow they found out that I was relocated to Waltham. The article listed the names of each of the men I killed, and scattered throughout it were quotes from their families and state pols about what an outrage it was that I'd been released. The article used what had to have been the prison photo taken several months ago when I was transferred out of Cedar Junction to the medium security prison. I hadn't seen that photo before, but Christ I looked ghoulish in it.

I took the paper to the cashier and bought it also. I tried to cover up the photo on the front page, but it didn't much matter. I could tell from the cashier's eyes that she had already recognized me. She didn't say anything about it, though. According to a clock behind her it was already six-thirty. I left and made my way to one of the diners that was supposed to be open then.

When I got to the diner the door was still locked. The lights were on and inside I could see a deathly pale girl moving around listlessly as she pulled chairs off tables and prepared the place for opening. She must've known I was standing out there but didn't once look my way. After five minutes of this I knocked on the door hoping she'd let me in so I could get out from the cold. She stared in my direction for a moment as if it pained her greatly to do so, her eyes boring through me instead of looking at me and, showing how much she was being put upon to make the gesture, indicated that it would be one more minute. It ended up being ten more before she unlocked the door. Up close she was younger than I first thought, probably no older than twenty. Her lipstick and mascara were the same black that her hair had been dyed, with the mascara applied thickly enough around her eyes to make a small lone ranger's mask. I'd seen fishing tackle boxes with less hooks in them than what she had pierced through her face. Mumbling, she thanked me for my patience, her voice flat, barely hiding its sarcasm.

It was clear from the way she looked at me that she had no idea who I was, which I was grateful for. It was too early in the morning to see any more fear and revulsion in a stranger's face. Just being seen as an anonymous old man was a relief. I followed her into the diner and she mumbled for me to take whichever table I wanted, and I took one far enough from the front window so that anyone walking by and looking in wouldn't be able to recognize me.

When she returned with a menu, I waved it off. I'd had enough time standing outside to have already memorized the one that had been posted by the front window, and I ordered black coffee, poached eggs, corned beef hash and pancakes; a breakfast I'd been dreaming about for years while in prison. Before she could move away from me I also asked for a yellow pages directory. Her eyes dulled to show how much of a burden this was, but when she came back with the coffee she also brought the phone book. Whenever she and the short-order cook weren't looking I discreetly ripped pages out of the phone book that I needed. I would've asked her for a piece of paper and pen instead, but I didn't want her feeling any more put upon.

When the food was brought over I started salivating at the sight and smell of it. It was just greasy-spoon stuff, but at that moment I don't think anything ever tasted better to me. I started shoveling the food in without even realizing it. Then I caught her smirking at me. Embarrassed, I turned away from her while I wiped some egg yolk off my chin, then forced myself to slow down and eat more leisurely. It wasn't easy. You get conditioned after so many years in prison to wolf your food down. When I was done I almost ordered another breakfast. Instead though, I sat and read the newspaper, asking for refills on my coffee whenever I could get the waitress over. By this time a few more people had wandered into the diner. I had my back to them, I don't think any of them recognized me. At least I couldn't feel any of them staring at me.

The third time I tried getting a refill the waitress told me I was only entitled to two with a cup of coffee. From the way her lips had curled into a tiny smirk I knew that wasn't a rule of the diner, just something she was making up for me. I told her I'd order another cup then, and a piece of apple pie along with it.

"We don't have pie this early."

"Then a doughnut. Jelly-filled."

There was still no recognition on her part, she just wanted me to leave the table. The place was mostly empty, but the way she was keeping at arm's length and had wrinkled her nose, it was probably because of the way I smelled, which surprised me. Not because I didn't smell, but that she could pick up my body odor over the dense musk perfume she had doused herself with.

She looked like she wanted to tell me they didn't have any

doughnuts either, but she didn't. Instead she left and came back ten minutes later with the doughnut and a fresh cup of coffee. This time I stretched things out further. By eight o'clock the diner had gotten crowded. A couple of blue-collar types stood nearby glowering at me as they waited for me to vacate my table, but they were wasting their efforts. I was just finishing up my first refill on the new cup and waiting for the waitress so I could get my second. I didn't leave the diner until after nine o'clock. I wanted to make sure the stores I needed to go to would be open before I left.

After I stepped outside I pulled from my pocket all of the pages from the phone book that I had crammed in there, then squinted at them until I could make out the addresses I needed. I was going to need a phone, at least for a little while, and I walked three blocks to a shop where for sixty bucks I bought a disposable cell phone with more calling minutes than I was going to need. The salesman tried selling me other services, like texting and music downloads, and I listened patiently until he gave up and finally accepted that he wasn't going to get any more money out of me. I was impressed with his initiative, though. You'd have thought with the way I smelled he'd be anxious to just close the deal on the phone purchase and herd me out of the store.

Once I was outside again, I found a quiet spot and played around with the phone until I figured out how to use it, then I took out those phone book pages again and called a mattress store. I negotiated the cheapest price I could and arranged to have the bed delivered by six, telling the salesman I'd pay cash instead of using a credit card. When he asked for a name, I made one up, and when he asked for my address I froze for a few moments before I was able to find the form I'd brought with me that had it on it. I guess the salesman must've taken it as a senior moment.

With the bed ordered and the little money I had dwindling fast, I next walked to a hardware store where I bought what I needed to clean my apartment, then I lugged the stuff back to the apartment building. I was out of breath by the time I got back and rested for a while before getting to work. It took several hours before I was done. I don't think it was possible to get the apartment really clean, but at least I knocked a good deal of the grime off of it. I went out again after that and bought several bath towels, soap, shampoo, and other personal hygiene items. When I returned to the apartment, I stripped and took a shower. The water never got hotter than lukewarm, but I stood under the shower head for a good hour trying to scrub those fourteen years of prison off of me.

After leaving the shower I brushed my teeth hard enough with a new toothbrush that my gums were bleeding up a small river in no time. I'd gotten used to shaving in prison without looking at myself, and I did it once more as I tried hard not to catch even a glimpse of myself in the mirror. When I was done with that I poured on some cheap cologne hoping it would hide the stench that had gotten embedded in my clothing. Then I got dressed and headed out.

It was a little before three o'clock. There wasn't much foot traffic, but there were plenty of cars once I got back on to Moody Street. I tried not to look, I tried to keep my focus straight ahead, but I could sense the occasional car slowing down to get a better look at me. I could feel the driver's eyes on me. It didn't happen often, maybe with four cars, but it was enough to get my heart pounding. I veered off Moody Street first chance I had and walked side streets as much as I could. I had to stop a couple of times to ask directions. In one of the stores the guy behind the cash register recognized me right off and after giving me a slow look up and down told me to go fuck myself. The other people I asked never bothered to get a good enough look at me to recognize me. The first three of them ignored me, the fourth gave me directions, talking loudly as if I were hard of hearing. I don't know why she thought that, but I didn't bother correcting her.

My first stop was at a bedding store where I bought sheets, a pillow and a blanket. After that I went to a thrift store where I was able to buy some used clothing very cheaply that fit better than what I had on. Three pairs of pants, same number of shirts, and a heavy wool sweater. The stuff smelled of mothballs, but that was an improvement on how my other clothes were smelling. I also bought a portable radio, a Red Sox cap and a pair of dark sunglasses. I put on the cap and pulled it down low, then the sunglasses, figuring that it might help disguise me. The way the lady working the cash register chatted with me it must've at least worked with her.

I was too loaded up with packages to drag the stuff back to my apartment, and I asked the woman if she could call me a taxi. She was more than happy to, and as I stood waiting for it she kept chatting away. I didn't pay attention to what she was saying. I wasn't used to that much talking. It was probably the most anyone had talked to me since prison, and maybe well before that. Anyway, all she accomplished was making my headache worse.

When the cab mercifully arrived, the driver sat where he was while I made two trips to carry out my packages. He didn't bother to hide his disappointment when I gave him my address. He wasn't going to make much money on this, and from the looks of me – especially given that he was picking me up at a thrift shop – he knew he wasn't going to get much of a tip. After a few minutes I noticed him studying me in the rear-view mirror.

"You're him," he said.

I didn't bother answering. I just looked out the window and tried to pretend he wasn't talking to me.

"You're him," he repeated, unperturbed by my ignoring him. "You're the one in the papers."

I felt my ears reddening. "So what," I found myself muttering.

"Speak up. I can't hear you."

I faced forward and found myself staring hard at the back of his head. "So what," I said again, louder this time.

"So maybe you can give me your autograph?"

The reddening in my ears had spread to my cheeks. At least it felt that way from the hotness. "Why the fuck would you want that?" I half-heard myself asking him.

He shrugged. "It might be worth money someday. I'll tell you what, you give me your autograph and the fare will be on me."

I didn't say another word to him. When he pulled up to my building the meter read three dollars and forty cents and I counted out exact change and pushed it through the slot in the Plexiglas separating us. His thick eyelids lowered in response. He watched me pull my packages out of the cab, waiting until I had them all out and was loaded up before calling out to me, telling me how he hoped they would catch up with me and in the end I'd get mine. Maybe the "they" he was referring to were Lombard's organization, maybe it was the families of my victims. I wasn't sure which it was, but in either case, I couldn't much argue with him, and didn't bother turning around.

It was five o'clock by the time I was back in my apartment. While I waited for the bed to be delivered I took inventory of the money I had left. Putting aside the hundred fifty dollars that the bed was going to cost me, I had eight hundred and forty-two dollars, and I still had more things I needed to buy. Still, even after that I should be left with five hundred, which would be enough to let me live somewhat decently for a month, and then I'd be on Theo's budget. I thought briefly about trying my luck at the track, see if I could boost what I had, but realized the futility of that. In my old days I made money that way, but it was because I was connected and the tips I was given were usually good. Anyway, a month would probably be enough time for me.

While I waited I took out my cell phone and tried to work up the courage to call Michael and Allison. It had been over two years since the last time I tried, and maybe they'd had a change of heart. In the end I couldn't do it. I had Michael's number keyed in on the phone, but all I could do was stare at it until a hard knocking on the door brought me out of my trance. I flipped the phone off and opened the door enough to see that the delivery men were there with my bed.

They set the new bed up quickly. The lead delivery man presented me with a bill, and while I counted out the cash he looked at me with a puzzled expression and then at his work order form which had the name I'd made up earlier.

"I could swear I know you," he said.

"Just one of those faces," I said.

His forehead wrinkled as he tried to dredge out where he knew me from. As he and his partner turned to leave, I reminded them about how they were supposed to remove the old bed. I couldn't blame them for the lack of enthusiasm they showed at the prospect of that – I wouldn't want to have to pick up and carry that damn mattress out either, at least not without several layers of protective clothing on. As they removed the mattress, the lead guy called out to me to let me know that he was sure he'd seen me before and he'd remember later. I closed the door on him without saying a word, deciding that I didn't want to ruin his surprise.

It was six o'clock. I felt bone-tired again, just like I had the other day. I wasn't used to this type of activity and schedule yet, but maybe more than that, it wore me down worrying about people recognizing me and waiting for that look they'd give me afterwards once they did. It was harder than I thought it would be. All those years that I worked for Lombard as a hit man I operated in the shadows. As far as my wife and kids were concerned, I worked in a liquor store. As far as my neighbors went, I was just someone who blended into the background.

I almost lay down on the new bed. I wanted to badly, but I knew if I did I'd tumble into a deep sleep and miss work. It didn't make sense for me to care that much about it since my expenses were basically covered for the next month, which was about as far ahead as I needed to worry about, but for some reason the job did seem to matter. Maybe it was the structure of it; giving me someplace to be, and in some small way allowing me to contribute to society. Or maybe it was simply finally doing something that my pop would be proud of. Whatever it was, I didn't want to lose it.

I loaded batteries into the portable radio I'd bought earlier, and brought it with me as I left the apartment. Once outside, I navigated again to Moody Street and found a cheap restaurant where I could get something to eat and drink enough coffee to keep me awake.

chapter 9

1973

A week before I'm supposed to be marrying Jenny, Vincent DiGrassi meets me about a contract he needs taken care of. He knows I'm getting married, and I ask him how urgent this is.

"Very," he tells me.

Oh, Christ. This is just what the fuck I need. With Jenny going nuts over all the wedding details, all the last-minute changes, her family coming in for the wedding, and all the other bullshit in my life right then.

"I am getting married…" I start to tell him.

"Maybe," he says, interrupting me, his eyes little more than what you'd see in a dead fish, his lips wire-tight. "In a week you could be going to a wedding, could be a funeral, all depends on you doing a clean, quick job on this one, or maybe instead you being stupid and thinking you can give me some grief."

He tries staring me down, but I can see the worry in his face no matter how hard he's trying to hide it. I don't know who this guy is that DiGrassi wants me to take out, but whoever he is he has DiGrassi worried.

We continue our staring contest for another ten or so

seconds. DiGrassi blinks first. His rock-hard expression melting a bit, he tells me, "Lenny, if you have to postpone your wedding, you gotta do it. This has to take priority, and that comes straight from the top. But there'll be a bonus in this for you, more than enough to make up for any inconvenience."

I look again at the name DiGrassi gave me. I don't know the guy. If he's in the game, I'm clueless how.

"Who is this guy?" I ask.

DiGrassi regains his ice-cold demeanor. "Why the fuck does that matter to you?"

I shrug, tell him it doesn't.

He starts to leave, stops himself to warn me to be careful with this one. Those little worry lines are once again cracking his icy exterior. After six hits all done without worry or fuss, this is the first time he suggests to me about being careful. I wonder briefly what's up with that.

That was four days ago. I know Jenny is furious about me leaving town. I gave her some bullshit reason and I've talked to her a few times over the phone since then, and she's not at all happy. If it wasn't for all the travel arrangements her relatives had made, she probably would've called off the wedding. That's how pissed she is.

This guy I've been after has been tough to get close to. He's careful, cautious. Maybe he knows about the contract on him, maybe it's just his nature. And to make my job even harder, I can't leave anything behind. His body has to disappear, no trace, no evidence of a killing.

After four days I finally have my opening. Security on his house is tight, and he keeps a Rottweiler loose in his yard so the damn thing will bark up a storm if anyone goes near the property. Earlier I took the dog out quietly, the silencer muffling the shot, the dog dying before he could get out as much as a whimper. That was hours ago. Now it's late and I've been standing in the shadows outside his home. Until twenty minutes ago I'd been hoping I wouldn't have to go in and massacre his whole family. It's so much damn harder to make a whole family disappear.

I don't have to do that any more. Twenty minutes ago he left the main house and entered a converted workshop in the back of an attached garage. Now he's using a hacksaw on something, I can't tell exactly what. With the lights off in the house it means his family is in bed. Yesterday evening when one of his kids had that Rottweiler out for a walk, I used the opportunity to tamper with one of the windows in the garage.

He's had his back turned to me the last ten minutes, and I've opened the window enough so I can slide the barrel of the gun underneath. Two silenced shots is all it takes. I open the window all the way and crawl in, taking in with me the duffel bag filled with chemicals that I've brought.

It turns out he's been using the hacksaw to cut off both barrels of a shotgun. That gets me curious. I start searching his workshop, and I find a false wall. Hidden inside is a large arsenal loaded with knives, guns and rifles of all different calibers, stacks of extra magazines, and even a few hand grenades. This makes me even more curious about my target.

I take some choice weapons out of the arsenal, then fit the false wall back in place. Then I go to work. He has his car keys on him which saves me from having to break into the car. I wrap his body with a plastic sheet that I had folded in my duffel bag and dump it in the trunk, then use the chemicals I brought to erase any forensic evidence. When I'm done I fix the lock on the window leaving it as good as new.

I open the garage door as quietly as possible so I can retrieve the Rottweiler's body and dump it in the trunk also. Earlier I'd cleaned up the area where I'd shot the dog as best I could. If someone starts looking for blood there they'll find it, but then again, why should anyone? What's more likely, that the guy left in the middle of the night and took his dog with him, or someone like me is able to kill the two of them and scrub the garage clean without anyone hearing it? The chances of anyone finding that dog's blood in the yard aren't too likely.

The property is on enough of an incline so that after I roll the dead man's car out of the garage I can coast it down to the end of the driveway, and only then turn over the engine. I have a long night ahead of me. I still have to dispose of the bodies, then have the car chopped up at one of Lombard's garages, but once I'm done with it I'm finished. The car I drove over with is parked several blocks away. I had stolen it earlier and cleaned it before leaving, so I can let it sit where it is.

Yeah, I might have a long night ahead of me, but I can't help smiling. By morning I'll be driving home, and the wedding will still be on as planned. Jenny might be mad for another day or two, but by Saturday my taking off the way I did will be forgotten.

I can't help wondering about the arsenal this guy had, that I caught him in the middle of making a sawed-off shotgun, and the whole urgency of this on Lombard's part. I can't stop wondering who the fuck this guy is.

It takes some effort, but I force my mind off of it. If DiGrassi wanted me to know that, he would have told me. Besides, I have a wedding to think about.

chapter 10

present

When I showed up at work, the same kid from the night before was at the front security desk. He handed me the office keys and tried hard to look through me, acting as if I weren't there. He might've been able to pull off this air of contempt but a tightness around his mouth betrayed him, showing how uneasy he was. I tried to think of something to say to put him at ease, but couldn't come up with anything. What was I going to tell him? That I was over sixty now, a changed man, and too conflicted over what I'd done in the past to even consider any more violence in my life? Fuck it, it would've been a waste of breath. In the end, neither of us said a word to the other.

Like the other day, I started on the bathrooms first. I had my portable radio set up on the cleaning cart and tried listening to music, but I found my mind kept drifting. It didn't help that my dinner had left me sluggish. I'd had my first cheeseburger and fries since being arrested, and while I'd poured a pot of black coffee down my throat, I'd also had my first beers in fourteen years and I was feeling the effects of them. To keep my mind focused and off the thoughts that kept trying to sneak in, I tuned in to a talk show.

For the first hour they had an author on talking about his latest book. The guy had a thick Irish brogue and it was interesting enough to keep me distracted. I still felt myself moving sluggishly, but at least I was distracted. After the segment with the author finished, I sobered up instantly from the effects of my greasy dinner and two beers when in the next segment they started discussing my release from prison. At first it was tough listening to what they were saying, but after a while I hardened to it. The comments from the people calling in were what you'd expect; what a travesty it was that the state would make any deal that allowed me to walk out of prison. One caller had to point out my ethnicity, claiming that I wasn't a full-blooded Italian, that my mother had been Jewish, as if that had anything to do with it. Another talked about my pop, how he knew him years ago, and how he was a good man who must be rolling around in his grave now over what I'd done.

The show attracted a few callers who tried to sound like tough guys. These wannabes speculated about how I must have a death wish staying in the area, hinting that there were enough people with grudges against me that I'd be turned into a grease spot soon enough. They tried to sound as if they were in the game, but they weren't. No one from Lombard's organization would've called that show.

About forty minutes into it, a woman's voice stopped me cold. She was talking about how much pain and suffering I had caused, her voice soft and halting as if she were on the verge of breaking down. I was pretty sure it was my daughter, Allison. I hadn't heard her voice since she was eighteen, and she'd be thirty-two now, but I was pretty sure it was her. I stood frozen for a minute listening to her, then realized I'd been holding my breath the whole time. I moved quickly to the cleaning cart and turned off the radio. My heart was pounding a mile a minute.

For a long time I couldn't move. I just kept playing her voice back in my head, replaying everything she had said as I tried to figure out if that caller had been my daughter. In the end I just wasn't sure. I almost took out my cell phone with the thought of calling Allison, but I couldn't do it.

That night I finished up a few minutes before two. Again, no words were spoken between me and the security guard when I checked in the keys. I wasn't so much tired when I walked back to my apartment – it was more like listlessness. It was desolate at that hour. No traffic sounds, no sight of anyone else. I couldn't shake this uneasiness in my gut, like I was walking through a graveyard. And I just couldn't get that woman's voice out of my head. The one who might've been Allison.

Later when I dropped on to my bed, I don't know if I fell asleep or drifted into some sort of unconsciousness, but whichever it was, I was grateful for the reprieve it gave me from all the thoughts buzzing through my head.

It was two days later that I caught the mouse that had been running around my apartment. I had left a mostly empty peanut butter jar on its side, and when I heard something clattering around inside it, I flipped the jar over. My original plan was to drown the damn thing in the toilet, but when I saw it on its hind legs with its front paws frantically scratching at the inside of the jar, I had a change of heart. Instead I got dressed, put my sweater and jacket on, and carried the jar to a small park four blocks away where I let it down on the grass. After the mouse scurried away from me, I tossed the jar into a trash can and headed back to my apartment. I had just gotten on to Moody Street when my cell phone rang.

No one should've had my number. I took the phone out of my pocket and stared at it before flipping it open. I didn't say anything, I just stood quietly and listened to what sounded like static on the other end. Then a man's voice came over the phone and told me I was a dead man. He called me by name so there was no mistaking that it could've been a wrong number. I didn't say anything in response. There was another half a minute of static before a click sounded to show that he had hung up.

I'd been so absorbed by the call that I'd stopped paying attention to my surroundings. Usually I was more careful about letting my guard down like that, and I looked around quickly, noticing the cars driving past me and the other pedestrians walking about. A man in his forties seemed to notice me looking at him and stared back. I don't think he had noticed me before that, and I looked away from him. If anyone had been watching me out there, I couldn't spot them. After giving it some thought, I headed back to the store where I'd bought the cell phone.

The salesman who had sold me the phone wasn't there. I tried describing him to the salesgirl on duty. She was in her twenties, very thin, not very attractive. While I explained how I wanted to talk again to this salesman, she stared at me with a humoring expression.

"Sir, what seems to be the problem?" she said instead of answering my question, a plastic smile stuck on her face.

"Someone called me on my cell phone," I said. "I want to talk to the salesman who sold me this. I think he must've given my number out."

"I'm sure he didn't do that," she said.

"He had to've," I said. "I didn't give my number to anyone, and I was told my number wouldn't be published anywhere."

"Are you sure you didn't give someone your number and forget about it?" she asked, her smile and tone turning even more patronizing.

"That's not what happened."

She shrugged, her eyes glazing enough to show that she didn't believe me. "Maybe you called someone first and they got your number from caller ID?" she offered.

"The person knew my name," I said. "Nobody I called on this phone knows my name."

She held her hand out for my cell phone. I gave it to her and she checked the call log, frowning at what she saw. "Is this the call?" she asked. "Today at nine-twenty?"

"Yeah."

"The call shows up in the log as *unavailable*. There's no phone number attached." She handed me back my phone. "I'm sorry, there's nothing more I can do to help you with this."

"Of course there is. You can give me the name of the salesman who sold me this phone like I've been asking."

"I can't do that," she said, her tone losing some of its patience.

"The phone call I received was threatening," I said. "The person calling me threatened my life."

She blinked several times as she looked at me, at first not believing what I told her. Then it dawned on her who I was. Her plastic smile faded fast from her face, leaving fear floating in her now liquid eyes. Watching the transformation that came over her made me just want to get the hell out of there.

"I don't know who sold you the phone," she said, lying to me, her voice weak, shaky. She looked like she was on the verge of tears. Like she wanted nothing more than to bolt from the store. "If you'd like I could exchange your phone so you would have a new number."

I thought about it, but decided I'd rather keep the phone. If someone wanted to call me badly enough, let them. "That's okay," I told her. "I'll keep this one." I started towards the door. I wanted to get out of there before she passed out on me, which she looked like she was about to do. I could spend some mornings watching the store for when my salesman returned back to work, but it would probably be as big a waste of time as this was. I doubted whether he would've gotten a name for whoever it was he gave my number to. Even if he was able to describe the person to me, what good would it do? After fourteen years out of the game, odds were I wouldn't know him, and even if it was someone from the old days, so what?

I did get one useful piece of information out of this. Someone must've followed me to the store when I first bought the phone, which meant someone was keeping track of me. At least on that day they were.

On my way back to my apartment I stopped off at the diner I'd had breakfast at my first morning out of prison and every day since. The same waitress from before was working – the one with the thick black mascara painted on to match her dye-job and lipstick. She'd been on the job every morning I'd been there. She still didn't know who I was, but the last couple of days she had warmed up to me – at least enough where she had dropped the gag about only allowing me two refills with a cup of coffee. When she saw me walk in and take a table, her eyes sparkled like black polished glass and a thin smile twisted her lips.

She walked over to my table, leaned in close, and said softly enough so that only I could hear, "The old coot's back again."

"I've been called worse," I said.

"I'm sure you have," she said, her smile turning more playful. "I'd ask if you'd like your usual, but with senility and all, I doubt you'd remember what your usual was."

I sat back in my seat and arched an eyebrow at her. "Okay, I'll bite. What makes you so sure I'm senile?"

She looked around quickly to make sure no one could hear her. "This is your fourth straight day coming here. You obviously can't remember what the food tastes like."

I laughed at that, and the sound of it startled me. It was the first time I had laughed out loud in years. In my mind I'd imagined my laugh sounding completely different, not like the wheezing, crackling noise that ended up oozing out of me. I cut it off quickly.

"I've been eating a lot worse," I said. "And yeah, I'll have the usual."

She gave me a funny look, but nodded. "Corned beef hash, poached eggs and pancakes it is. If you're going to be coming here all the time, we might as well know each other's names so that I can quit calling you the *old coot*, not that it's not fitting. My name's Lucinda."

She offered me a small hand, her fingernails painted the same black as her lips, hair and eyes. I took it, felt the warmth of her skin. I almost gave her my real name, but I ended up telling her I was *Larry*.

"Larry, huh?" she said. "I guess we're both a couple of *L*s. Seems so fitting. I'll get your breakfast order in." She started to walk away but stopped to look over her shoulder at me. "You should laugh more," she told me. "It sounds like you're badly out of practice."

I watched as she walked away, and fought against the impure thoughts I was having about a girl younger than my own daughter. Once I remembered how I now looked and how old I was, those thoughts went away as fast as if a switch had been thrown. As if a bucket of ice water had been dumped on my head.

Like every other time I'd been there I was sitting with my back to the window so that passersby wouldn't be able to recognize me. I didn't hear him walk into the diner, and it caught me by surprise when he sat across from me. He was the same man I'd seen earlier after I'd gotten that phone call: the one who caught me looking in his direction and ended up staring back at me in response.

"Leonard March?" he said.

I didn't say anything. Instinctively I reached for the knife laid out in front of me. He noticed this movement, and I caught myself and pulled my hand back. We both sat staring at each other. He was balding, a thick build, and sloppily dressed with his jacket collar partially up and a polo shirt hanging loosely out of his pants. I knew he wasn't part of Lombard's organization – he was too soft-looking for it to be that. Almost as if a deck of cards were flipping through my mind, I tried to picture the faces of the men I had killed. Some of them were nothing more than a blur, most, though, I could see clearly. If this man was related to any of them, I couldn't figure it out.

"You have to be Leonard March," he said, nodding, satisfied. His tongue was thick and looked almost purple as it pushed out of his mouth and wetted his lips. He leaned forward so that his arms rested on the table. They were thick, heavy arms, but more fat than muscle.

"My name's Andy Baker," he said, an eagerness shining in his eyes. "I have a proposition for you."

He waited for me to say something. When I didn't, he appeared stuck for a few seconds as if things weren't going according to a carefully devised script. He wet his lips again, said, "I'm a writer. I want to write a book with you."

That wasn't what I was expecting. I gave him a hard look, trying to figure out if this was some line or if he was serious.

"How long have you been following me?" I asked.

"What? No, I haven't been following you. When I heard on the news about you living in Waltham, I drove down here this morning hoping to spot you, but no, I haven't been following you. Just serendipity, that's all."

"You didn't call me on my cell phone this morning?"

He looked confused. "Call you on your cell phone? What

are you talking about? How would I've gotten your number?" He edged closer, said, "But I do want to write a book with you. The two of us can make a lot of money doing this, Mr March. Maybe a hundred grand each for the advance, a lot more if the book does well."

I sat quietly appraising him. He was serious, but he was also talking out of his ass. He didn't have a book deal. Even if he did, though, I wouldn't have had any interest. Even if I could've kept the money instead of paying it all out after the wrongful death suits went to court, I wouldn't have had any interest.

"I have some advice for you," I said.

"What?"

"Next time you want to talk business with someone, ask if you can sit at their table. Don't just force your way in like an asshole."

At first his expression was blank. Once he comprehended what I said, hurt showed on his mouth. He pushed himself a few inches from the table.

"I'm sorry if I was rude, but I've been talking to publishers, and the money I'm telling you about is real."

"All I want is for you to get up from my table and walk away."

It was like all the air had been let out of a tire the way he seemed to deflate right in front of me. He stood up, took a couple of aimless steps away from me, then fished a business card out of his pocket and spun on his heels like a drunk man so he could drop the card on the table in front of me.

"When you change your mind, call me," he said. "There's too much money in this for you not to change your mind."

He stood silently staring at me, a shrewdness slowly taking over his expression. "I've read enough about you to know what your financial situation is," he continued. "And besides, this would give you a chance to get your story out in your own words instead of how the media is portraying you."

I pocketed his card for no other reason than to get him to leave. He was wrong. As far as the media went, I'd been getting off easy. The last thing I wanted was for people to be able to read what really happened. The bare sketches that the newspapers provided were bad enough, but not nearly as ugly as what the real truth was. I had no excuses and no reasonable explanations for the things I did.

He smiled when he saw me put his card away. He took several steps away before turning back to face me again, this time warning me not to try to cut him out. "Everyone thinks they can write a book these days," he told me, accusingly. "It's bullshit, which is why the market is flooded with so much crap."

With that he finally left. I twisted my body around enough so I could watch him walk out the door. When I turned back around, I noticed Lucinda standing a few tables away holding a coffee pot, her eyes fixed on me.

"What was that all about?" she asked me.

Her complexion before had been on the pale side, now it looked almost bone-white in contrast to all of her goth shading. I wondered briefly how much of the conversation she had heard. All I knew was that she had heard enough to freak her out a bit.

"The guy's a nut," I said. "I never saw him before. He just came in and sat at my table, then started rambling on about some nonsense."

She walked over and poured me a cup of coffee, her mouth compressed tightly. It wasn't until she moved away that she asked me about the book the guy was talking about. "Why was that?" she asked, her eyes scrunching suspiciously. "Are you someone famous or something?"

I shook my head. "You got me right the first time. These days I'm not much more than an old coot. No one worth paying attention to."

I saw a flicker of doubt in her eyes as she walked away. While I waited for my breakfast, I drank the black coffee Lucinda had poured me and chewed on a few aspirin. My headache had gotten worse the last few minutes.

When Lucinda brought my food over she was closer to her usual acerbic self. Not a hundred percent, but closer. It didn't help me any. I'd already lost my appetite.

chapter 11

1977

Vincent DiGrassi tells me I have a choice. "This one's not family business," he tells me. "So you don't got to take it." He pauses for a moment to take a healthy swig of Pepto-Bismol, then continues, "Lenny, it's not gonna be the way you usually do business. It's risky. But if you do it, there's a ten grand bonus in it for you."

Ten grand will help right now. Jenny's pregnant with our second kid, and we just bought a house in Revere, and then there's all this new furniture Jenny wants. I have DiGrassi explain it to me, and when he does I almost walk away from it. Risky isn't even close to what this is. If it weren't for that extra ten grand…

"What the hell," I tell him. "A job's a job, even one as fucked up as this one. Mr DiGrassi, you on a diet these days? It looks like you shed a few."

He nods. "Yeah, I'm on a diet. It's called the sonofabitch heartburn diet. Sal's going to be grateful you doing this, Lenny. Both the money part of it and that it don't hurt to have that prick in Southie owing us a favor. And he's going to be owing us big for this."

"Yeah, he will. At least if his information is on the level. I wonder how he got tipped off?"

DiGrassi shrugs. It not that important to him. I collect what I need from him and leave.

That was hours ago. Now I'm driving a stolen car to every hole-in-the-wall bar in Charlestown looking for my target. I'm dressed in a blond wig with matching fake blond mustache and beard glued on. Under the seat next to me is a 9mm automatic. Each bar I go to it's the same thing; at this hour nothing but a few degenerate alkies scattered around. According to our client in Southie, my target, one Douglas Behrle, is supposed to be hiding out in Charlestown before meeting with the Feds at four o'clock. Supposedly Behrle wants to turn rat and I have to ice him before he has the opportunity.

I'm reaching the point where I'm about to give up. It's past three o'clock already and who knows how good the information is. Probably old bullshit, or maybe Behrle planned to hang out in Charlestown and had a change of heart. Who the fuck knows where he is now? There's any number of towns around here where he could be killing an afternoon sucking down beers in a dive bar.

I hang an illegal U-turn on Monument Avenue, and that's when I spot Behrle with two other guys, all of them getting into a Datsun sports coupe. I know it's Behrle, I have his picture on the seat next to me. Medium-height, beanpole thin, pronounced Adam's apple, acne-scarred face. I have no clue who the guys are with him. They could be Feds, could be other Southie guys. It doesn't matter. I slam the Buick Regal I'm driving into the side of their Datsun. While they're still collecting themselves and trying to figure out what happened, I jump out of the car with the 9mm in hand, first popping the two guys with Behrle, then Behrle himself. It all takes no more than thirty seconds. With the way his brains are leaking out of his skull, Behrle's gotta be dead, no question. The other two should be dead, and it would be tragic for them if they weren't given the way I'm leaving them, but in either case it doesn't much matter.

Without bothering to look around for witnesses, I race back to my car and drive off. The next ten minutes are going to be the trickiest. If anyone calls in my car and the police run into me I'll be earning every penny of that ten grand bonus.

I work my way off Monument Ave., driving away from the Bunker Hill monument before circling back using side streets, then finding the alley where a car's waiting for me. No cops, no one following me. Sinking low in my seat, I take the wig off, then use an adhesive remover to get the fake beard and mustache off. I pull off the flowered Hawaiian shirt I'm wearing and slip on a gray tee shirt. The shirt, fake beard, mustache, wig, 9mm go into a bag, and I take it with me when I move to the Ford Pinto waiting for me. I wait until I get into the Pinto before I take off my driving gloves and drop them in the bag also.

When I drive out of the alley there are no cops, nothing. I start to relax. I rub a hand across my face and feel the coarseness of the glue still stuck there. Before I get home to Jenny I'll have to make sure I have it all off.

It's not until I'm driving over the Tobin Bridge that I hear a radio report about the brazen massacre of three men on Monument Avenue done within the hour in broad daylight. I can hear police sirens off in the distance, but no one's after me. I wonder again how our client in Southie knew about Behrle wanting to rat him out to the Feds. I can't help wondering who tipped him off.

chapter 12

present

The weekend was uneventful. My headaches were bad, but that was nothing new. Saturday night the same kid was working the security desk, and like the other times we didn't say one word to each other, but I was beginning to prefer it like that. I made it through the night listening to a classic rock station without my mind wandering too much, which was about all I could ask for.

I had Sunday off, and I ended up buying a recliner, lamp and a few other odds and ends at a garage sale. The guy I bought the stuff from had a pickup truck, and for an extra ten bucks he agreed to help me move it all to my apartment. He didn't recognize me, and acted both friendly and deferential as if I were some grandfatherly type. He kept asking me with genuine concern if I was okay while I carried my end of the recliner. It was funny in a way since he was breathing harder and was more red-faced from the effort than I was. Anyway, all of the stuff, including the extra ten bucks that I kicked in, ended up only adding up to seventy-eight dollars. The recliner, while a good twenty years old and kind of beat-up with its fabric stained and torn in spots, was comfortable. At least I had a good set-up now for reading.

There was nothing about me in Saturday's paper. The Sunday paper had an article about me buried in the Metro section, and this time there were no pictures. Both Saturday and Sunday I went to the same diner for breakfast that I'd been going to every morning. It turned out Lucinda didn't work weekends, which I was disappointed about. The waitress working in her place was a stout gray-haired woman in her fifties and just as surly as Lucinda had been that first day, but at least she didn't recognize me. Not too many people seemed to. A few did, I could tell from their rubbernecking, and from the shift in their expression – from curiosity to something more like fear, but probably no more than ten people the whole weekend, at least as far as I could tell. None of these people bothered saying anything to me. Some would just move faster to get away from me, others would slow down to get a better look, but not a single word from any of them.

Sunday afternoon I thought about going to the horse track to try to parlay my dwindling funds into something more substantial, at least that's what I tried telling myself. The truth was I missed going to the track. It wasn't even the gambling as much as watching the horses. They were such magnificent animals. At one point I had dreamed of owning a race horse. I'd had enough money socked away where I could've done it, but then I would've had to explain to Jenny how I came up with all that money working at a liquor store. And Lombard would not have been happy with me doing something like that. Part of the deal had been for me to keep a low profile.

In the end I skipped going to the track and went to a free movie at the library instead. Too many people would've recognized me if I had gone to the track, and they were people better off not recognizing me.

It wasn't until Monday morning when my cell phone rang again. Like before, the caller ID indicated the source of the call was *unavailable*. I let it ring through without answering it. Five minutes later when the phone rang again, I flipped it open and asked who was calling. At first there was nothing but static, then a man's voice telling me to enjoy life while I still could. It sounded like it could've been the same voice I had heard before, but I wasn't sure.

"You're such a tough guy," I said. "Why don't you tell me this face to face."

There was another long static-like silence where I wasn't sure whether he had hung up. Then, "You'll be seeing me soon enough, March," and then a click as he ended the call.

Before that, I had been up for hours sitting in my recliner reading one of the books I had taken out of the library. I had a large stack of them piled up next to my chair. As I mentioned before, it was the best way I knew to kill those early morning hours and keep past memories at bay. It was a little past nine o'clock and the call had left me no longer in the mood to do any more reading. I got up and headed to the bathroom where I showered as much of the grime off of me as I could, then doused myself with cheap cologne. Each day the stench of prison was getting a little bit less. I could still smell it on me, but it took more of an effort now.

Lucinda was back at work Monday morning. At ten o'clock when I arrived there the place was mostly empty, and she gave me a wink on seeing me. Later, when I ordered French toast and sausage instead of my usual breakfast, she put her hands to her chest as if she were having a heart attack, then showed me a wry smile, commenting on how my brains were too scrambled to remember my "usual". She chewed the fat with me for a few minutes, and between her sarcastic cracks, she let on that she was thinking of going back for a GED degree, maybe even college someday. When she came back with a pot of coffee, any suspicions she might've had after overhearing that so-called writer the other day were long gone.

I was about to leave when this biker-type walked in, and the way he stared at Lucinda put me back in my seat. He was in his twenties, a big guy wearing a black leather biker's jacket, jeans, and biker boots. Tattoos decorated his neck and shaved skull.

Lucinda noticed him also and was trying to bravely stare him down, but I could see the worry creasing her brow. The guy walked up to her and grabbed her arm roughly. She tried to pull free but couldn't.

"You bitch," he said. "You gonna let me buy you drinks all night, then slip me like that? Fuck that."

I walked over to him and told him to let go of her. He stared at me as if I were nuts.

"Gramps, this is none of your business. Beat it before you hurt your hip."

"Let go of her or I'll break your fucking wrist."

That just annoyed him even more. He reached out to push me away. I stepped aside and grabbed him by his fingers and twisted them back until he fell to his knees.

"You better fucking let go," he demanded. He was helpless in the position I had him in. I increased the pressure until tears came to his eyes.

"A little more pressure and your wrist snaps," I told him.

"I'm going to fucking kill you."

"Really? With two broken wrists? 'Cause after I break this one I'm breaking the other."

Lucinda had been watching this quietly. "Should I call the police?" she asked me.

"I don't think that's necessary." I addressed the guy on his knees, the one whose wrist I was nearly breaking. "How much did you spend on drinks last night?"

"Fifty bucks," he forced out.

With my free hand I took my wallet from my pocket and handed it to Lucinda. "Count out fifty dollars and give it to this scumbag." After she did that I told the guy he had two choices, accept the money and get the fuck out of there or have more than his wrist broken. I let go of him then.

He stood up holding his wrist as if I had broken it, which I hadn't. For a moment it looked like he wanted to take a swing at me, but instead he pocketed the money and called me a *fucking lunatic* before heading out the door. Lucinda stared at me with amazement. "I'm breathless right now," she said, and she sounded it.

She had me sit back down, and brought me over a piece of cherry pie and a fresh coffee. I sat for a while eating while she kept me company. When I told her I better get going, she looked worried.

"He might be out there looking for you," she said.

"Nah, he's a coward." I hesitated, then asked, "Whatever possessed you to let someone like that buy you drinks?"

She smiled at that. "I ended up ditching him, didn't I?"

I couldn't help smiling back at her. I nodded to her as I left the diner. I looked around to see if he was out there waiting for me, but I guess he had better sense than to be waiting for a lunatic.

Later that morning I went back to the store that sold me my cell phone, but the salesman I had dealt with still wasn't there. The only person working in the store was the same salesgirl I had tried talking to earlier, and she looked horrified when she saw me walk back into the place. I didn't bother talking to her, and instead just turned around and left.

It was a warmish October day and the sun felt good on my face. With nothing else to do, I took a walk down some side streets and ended up stumbling upon the Charles River. I walked along it until I found a grassy spot where I could sit and watch the water. My pop used to tell me how he swam in the Charles River when he was growing up, but by the time I was a kid the river had gotten too polluted for anything like that. Not only was it a yellowish brown color but you could smell the chemicals and sewage that came off of it. Now as I sat there the water looked clean. I wondered briefly whether it actually was or if it was an illusion with the muck and filth still there but better hidden beneath the surface.

Looking out over the water, my thoughts slowly drifted to Jenny. She had to know early on that I was involved in some sort of shady business. We had too nice a home and too many other nice possessions for me to have just been working at a liquor store, and she was too smart not to know I couldn't've made all that extra money betting on the horses like I used to tell her I did. I'm sure she never suspected me of being a hit man, but she knew something was up. There were those times I'd catch her giving me an odd look before she'd realize it and correct it. And then there were those times when I would need to leave town for days or longer, and those questions she'd swallow back when I would return home. It must've crushed her when she found out the truth, but even then she tried to hide it from me and put a brave face on. She never abandoned me, and right up until the end before cancer got her, I knew she would've been waiting for me if she could've.

It was hard thinking of her dying the way she did. I knew it had been a long, painful death for her. My mom had written me several letters letting me know what Jenny went through. Even through all of that, Jenny acted cheerfully the few times I was able to reach her by phone, trying to pretend there was nothing wrong with her.

When she finally succumbed I didn't know about it until

months afterwards. By this time my mom had already been dead for six months, and I had no contact with my kids. I guess the prison officials left responsibility for informing me about my wife to my kids, or maybe things just slipped through the cracks. Even at this late date I didn't know where Jenny was buried, but I guess it didn't much matter. It wasn't her there, just some bones left from her. It wouldn't make any difference if I visited the grave or not. Nothing could change that she was gone.

I tried hard to remember what my wife looked like, but I could only bring up a vague impression. It had been years since I'd been able to picture how Jenny looked. I had little to console myself over what happened with her other than I'd been able to tell her where my safety deposit boxes were without the federal or state officials ever having any idea about them. At least she had been able to live out her last few years in comfort before the cancer hit her, and my kids were able to go to college.

After a while I found that I had stopped thinking of Jenny, and instead my thoughts had moved on to my victims. It wasn't so much that I was trying to make peace with what I had done as trying to understand how I could've done what I did. I tried to make some sense of the person I was now and who I used to be and the brutality back then that I was capable of. I thought about the biker in Lucinda's diner whose wrist I almost broke, and wondered whether that meant anything, and decided it didn't. But even with who I was back then, I never once laid a finger on my wife or kids. They never once looked at me with fear or dread. I tried to put that in perspective with what I used to see in my victim's face before the last moment, but it exhausted me.

Eventually I gave up trying to make sense of it. Instead, I focused on just clearing my head and trying to think of nothing. More than anything I wanted to just lie back and enjoy the feel of the sun on my face. It didn't work. Too many memories pushed their way through, and before too long I had to get up in my attempt to outrun them, or at least outwalk them.

I spent the rest of the morning and a good part of the afternoon walking along the Charles River trying to leave those memories far behind, one in particular which especially haunted me. It was four o'clock when I returned back to Moody Street. I ate an early dinner at a Korean barbecue place. The prices were cheap and the food tasted good, and for the most part I was too tired to pay attention to those old memories. After a couple of beers it wasn't even an issue.

That night when I left work, I thought I again saw a black sedan following me. I had this impression that it had turned down a side street, but by the time I looked for it, it was gone, nothing but a mirage. I was bone-tired, especially after all the walking I'd done earlier, and decided my mind had to've been playing tricks on me – it wasn't as if I could actually remember hearing anything, or for that matter, seeing anything once I rubbed the exhaustion out of my eyes, but still, it left me feeling unsettled.

Tuesday turned out to be uneventful. It was especially quiet that morning at the diner and Lucinda ended up sitting down at my table and reading me prose from a notebook that she kept. When she asked me what I thought, I could see the anxiousness in her eyes and tugging at her mouth. I told her the truth, that I thought it was good, and she made a few cracks, both self-deprecating and insulting, about the state of my mental faculties if I thought that crap was any good and how ridiculous it was for her to care anyway about what a senile old coot like me thought, but I could tell it was a relief to her that I liked it, and she seemed to move lighter on her feet afterwards.

Later, I tried the phone store again, and my salesman still wasn't there. I spent the rest of the morning at the library searching through old newspapers. Eventually I found Jenny's obituary. It talked about her being a loving mother and sister, but nothing about being a loving wife. I was left out of it. I wished my kids had included a picture of Jenny with the notice. The only small bit of consolation I pulled out of it was I now knew where Jenny was buried.

I thought about why my kids had left her picture out of the obituary, and decided they had done it intentionally thinking that someday I'd be out of prison and I'd be looking for it. The day I found out about Jenny dying, I left messages with both Michael and Allison, asking if they could send me a picture of their mother since the ones I had brought to prison years earlier had disappeared from my cell. If my kids heard my messages, they didn't bother responding to them and I never received any pictures in the mail. To make matters even more pointless, the cemetery Jenny was buried in was in Revere and right in the middle of Lombard's territory. I wouldn't put it past them having someone watching Jenny's gravesite. Maybe when I know my time has run out, I'll make the trip. For now it wouldn't be safe for me to go there, and I wasn't about to commit suicide – at least not yet, and especially not by proxy.

That night I couldn't help feeling a heaviness in my chest as I cleaned the office building. I tried listening to music, but my mind kept wandering too much, and I ended up tuning into a talk show. More scandals had broken since I'd been released from prison. The big one that they talked about that night was the recent shooting involving a ball player at a local club. The ball player, who was unhurt, had supposedly been the target for the shooting but a bystander was the one who took a bullet in the neck and was now in critical condition and on life support.

The people calling into the talk show were speculating that the ball player had fired shots also, maybe even the one which wounded the bystander. I was quickly fading into yesterday's news.

When I walked home later, I tried to stay alert. The streets were empty and I didn't see any cars. No one was out there looking for me. I pretty much convinced myself that I must've been seeing things the other night.

It was twenty past two by the time I got back to my apartment. I almost called my son, Michael. I wanted to. I had the cell phone out and had keyed in his phone number, but in the end I flipped the phone shut. If I had made the call at that hour all I'd be doing would be giving him and his wife more ammunition to use against me. At least I had enough sense to realize that, and that was mostly why I didn't make the call, but I guess it was also partly that I hadn't worked up the nerve yet to do it.

chapter 13

1978

I'm stocking bottles of gin and vodka when a face from the past walks into the store. Joey Lando. It's been years since I've seen him, not since that day when we worked Ernie Arlosi over for fourteen hundred bucks and Joey ended up ratting me out to DiGrassi. I almost don't recognize him with how much fleshier he's gotten and the thick white scar running from his eye to his chin. The scar makes his flesh look uneven, almost as if he's wearing a piece of leather over part of his face. When he spots me a wide grin stretches his lips and there's no mistaking him.

He eyes me up and down, smirking, then walks over. It's a fluke that he catches me while I'm actually doing work. Every once in a while, I get restless and stock merchandise or handle the cash register or some other menial task. Mostly when I'm there I hang out in the backroom reading racing forms or magazines. It's lucky Joey walks in when he does; it helps convince him I'm just a blue-collar working stiff.

"I wouldn't believe it if I didn't see it with my own eyes," he says, still grinning his half-smirk. "Fuck, I thought they were just bullshit rumors. Lenny March working an honest job. Don't tell me it's true about you having a wife and kids also?"

"Yeah, it's true." I look past him to make sure no one's standing nearby. "I never thought I'd see your face again. Not after you ratting me out to Vincent DiGrassi."

"His boys give you a good beating, huh?"

"Yeah, I'd say so."

Joey points to the small circle of red puckered skin on my cheek. "You get that from him?"

I nod. "It was part of a test to see if I was a rat. I passed, I guess you and Steve didn't."

Joey's eyes dull a bit. He's still grinning but it's forced now. "I always regretted that," he says. "But you don't know what they were doing to us to make us talk." He runs a thumb over the full length of his scar. "And besides, you got off easy compared to Steve and me."

I soften as I look at him and remember the old days when we ran together. It's a shame that he and Steve fell apart the way they did when DiGrassi put them to the test, but I guess they just didn't have what it took.

"What do you want?" I ask.

"How about buying you a beer or two."

"No problem. The cooler's back against the wall. These days I'm drinking Michelob. You want to break up a six-pack, go for it."

He laughs. "Not here, Lenny. Someplace quiet where we can sit down and talk. How about it?"

"Where do you have in mind?"

"Connolly's Pub. One block down. What do you say?"

For years I had thought about looking him and Steve up and kicking the shit out of them. Those feelings have passed. Now I'm curious what he wants to talk about. Of course, I could leave with him now – no one here has me on a clock, but

I want to keep up the pretense of working a real job. I tell him I get off at six and I'll meet him then. He tells me he'll be there. After he leaves, I go back to stacking bottles. When I'm done, I head to the backroom and pick up the day's racing form. I was given a "can't miss" tip for later that night at Suffolk Downs, and figure I might as well play the rest of the ponies while I'm there.

I walk into Connolly's Pub at quarter past six and Joey's waiting at the bar, trying to look casual about it. He orders a couple of beers and we take them to a table in back.

"I still can't believe you're working a nine-to-five job," he says, shaking his head.

"Eight to six," I say, correcting him.

He takes a long pull on his Bud, wipes a hand across his mouth. "We ran together long enough back in the day. I know you, Lenny, I know what you're made of, and I don't buy that you can be happy living this bullshit life."

"People change."

"Not you." He's shaking his head angrily, takes another long pull at his Bud, emptying it. "Fuck, I saw first hand the things you used to do, and the look in your eyes when you did them. No one was a badder muthafucka in the day. And the guy I'm looking at now is the same fucking person. So don't feed me any bullshit about people changing."

He brings the Bud to his lips, realizes the bottle's empty and leaves the table. When he returns he has a couple of fresh beers; the Michelob he hands to me. His demeanor is calmer, more relaxed. He leans forward and asks me if I want to hear what he has to say. I nod. He edges even closer, his eyelids drop a quarter of an inch. He's got his back to the room while I'm facing it, but he knows I'll warn him if anyone comes nearby.

"The two of us, we can each make thirty grand next week," he says, his voice low enough that I have to strain to hear him.

"I told you before I'm out of the game."

"Sure you are." A thin smile creeps over his lips. He edges even closer so he's leaning halfway across the table. "You know those bank machines popping up all over the place? I've got someone on the inside giving me a schedule of when a certain bank refills theirs. When it's done, it's with twenties, about ten grand worth. Next week I'm going to hit ten banks, all within a three-hour span. By the time the bank realizes what's going on it will be too late for them to do anything about adding security."

"Why do you need me?"

"It's a two-man job." Joey's lids drop even further, the little I can see of his eyes is hard stone as they stare at me. "You got one guard in the armored truck, another reloading the machine. It's mostly a smash and grab, but you need someone keeping the guard in the truck occupied."

"What about your inside man?"

Joey makes a face. "It's a she, and no, she's not the one to do this with me."

"Problem is, neither am I. I've got a wife, kids, and a steady job. Sorry, Joey."

He smiles at me as if I'm kidding him. Slowly it wears off once he realizes I'm not, and what's left behind is the hard look of a stone-cold killer.

"You're full of shit," he tells me.

I shrug. "It's the way it is now."

"You're only kidding yourself. A fucking blind man can see that."

I don't say anything.

I can see the decision being made in his eyes on what he's going to do next. "Are you going to rat me out?" he asks.

"If I didn't back then to DiGrassi, I'm sure as fuck not going to do it now. Besides, I wouldn't want my wife knowing I used to hang out with people like you."

He accepts that. Without a word he gets up and walks out of the bar. I sit and finish my beer.

chapter 14

present

It had been a long time since I remembered dreaming. I knew I had dreams as a kid, but couldn't remember any since then, at least none since I was out of elementary school. That night I woke up from a doozy of one. More than that, the dream jolted me awake, and left me sweating through my underwear and sitting up fast in bed with my heart pounding so hard I could feel it in my temples.

The dream had me at a funeral home, stuck inside a room filled with coffins one stacked on top of the next. There was an unfamiliar man keeping me company. He looked almost like a cadaver himself with red rouge painted on his cheeks and sparse thin hair slicked back with grease. He was dressed in a black suit that was too small on him; it made his sleeves and pants legs pull up showing inches of his bony arms above his wrists and his white socks stretched high above his ankles. He stayed mute, refusing to say anything to me. I couldn't place ever seeing him before, but he acted as if he knew me.

"What am I doing here?" I asked him.

He smiled showing tiny baby teeth, and gestured that

I should look inside the coffins. I wanted to flee the room, I certainly didn't want to open up any of those coffins, but it was as if I had no choice. Almost like I was a marionette being controlled by strings. I struggled to unstack the coffins. It was hard work, back-breaking work, especially since I didn't want them falling and breaking open, but eventually I lowered them on to the floor and took the lids off. Inside were badly decomposed bodies. The stench was horrific. There wasn't much left of any of the corpses, only ragged skin covering their skulls and parts of their bodies, but somehow there was enough left of their faces so I could recognize them as the people I had killed.

There was one coffin that stood out from the others. This one was nailed shut. I counted the coffins I had looked in, and there were twenty-eight of them. I asked the man with me about the twenty-ninth coffin. Instead of answering me he just smiled, his skin stretching tight against his face and looking as thin as if it were paper.

"Am I supposed to be in that last coffin?" I asked him.

He shook his head sadly at me, as if I were supposed to know the answer. Still, though, his smile stretched tighter.

"Jenny?"

His smile stretched still tighter. The skin covering his cheeks began to rip exposing parts of his jaw through the opening. And still, he kept smiling.

I woke up then.

Christ, what a dream. If that's what they were like, I was grateful that was the first one I could remember in over fifty years. For a good ten minutes I sat silently before I trusted myself to move. Only after the pounding in my chest subsided did I pull myself off the bed and shuffle off to the bathroom to splash cold water over my face and dry the sweat off. I made sure not to catch a glimpse of myself in the mirror. I didn't want to risk seeing those same hollowed cheeks and dead sunken eyes that that man in my dream had.

It wasn't even three-thirty in the morning yet. I'd only been sleeping an hour. I was tired and needed more than that hour, but I didn't go back to bed. I didn't want to lie there thinking about what that dream meant, and I certainly didn't want to find myself slipping back into it. Instead I sat in my recliner and picked up a book that I'd been reading earlier in the day. At some point I dozed off. When I opened my eyes again sunlight was flooding the room. According to my alarm clock it was six o'clock. I had this vague image of lights being turned on and horns being blasted – almost as if I were back in prison, and for a few seconds I could smell that prison stench coming off me in waves. It was stronger than I had smelt it in days. I stumbled to the bathroom to try to scrub it off. I ended up standing in the shower for a half hour, and afterwards I slapped on enough cologne to hide any smell of prison that might've lingered.

That morning the diner was busy when I got there and I had to take a table near the front window. Lucinda was too busy running from table to table to do much more than give me a wink. Like every other morning, no one bothered looking at me. As far as the other customers were concerned I was just some invisible old man not worth paying any attention. That was what I liked most about the place, that, and Lucinda.

I was halfway through my French toast and bacon when a man sat down at my table facing me. It took me by surprise, and at first I thought it was the same wannabe writer from the day before. He looked similar; forties, heavy-set, balding. But he wasn't the same man. This one was glaring at me with a white-hot intensity. A thick ugly vein bulged from his forehead. Nothing but hatred in his face.

"You rotten piece of shit," he swore, his voice loud enough

so that everyone in the room could hear him. The din from the room faded fast after that. I could sense all eyes turned our way. I didn't want to look, but a glimpse showed Lucinda staring intently at us.

"Why don't we talk in private?" I offered.

"I don't think so," he said, his voice maybe even an octave louder and echoing through the now quiet diner. He smiled as he noticed how uncomfortable I was, then turned sideways to address the rest of the room.

"You've got a celebrity with you," he said. "Lenny March, mass murderer extraordinaire. The piece of shit they've been talking about in the news who killed twenty-eight people for the mob. The same one who murdered my dad."

When he first started his speech I felt a hotness flushing my face. That was gone now, replaced by something cold. Everything had gotten very still. The rest of the room seemed to dissolve as I stared back at this man, my voice odd and unnatural to me when I asked him who his pop was.

His lips curled as if he wanted to spit at me. What he spat out was the name, "Frank Mackey".

I nodded, remembering Mackey. "Your old man was quite a piece of work," I told him. "He used to do truck hijackings, but that wasn't why Lombard ordered the hit. Mackey grabbed a sixteen-year-old girl off the street, and held her for three days in the basement of an abandoned warehouse where he repeatedly fucked every body orifice this poor girl had. Her family wanted justice, but they also didn't want this girl humiliated any further by the police or the courts, so they appealed to Lombard."

What I said stunned him. "You're lying."

"Sorry, I'm not. Your old man was one of the few hits that I would've gladly done for free. Lombard wanted it to be more than just a hit. He wanted me to make sure there would have to be a closed casket, and more, he wanted your old man to suffer. And I did a hell of a job with it. Kept him alive for hours while I whittled away pieces of him. Now get the fuck away from my table. I'm eating."

His skin color had dropped to a milk-white. Any fury that had been raging in his eyes fizzled. He was unsure of himself, wondering how much of what I told him was true, although at some level probably realizing all of it was. I picked up my fork and continued eating my French toast. He sat across from me for another minute and made a few idle threats about how this wasn't over, but the steam had been taken out of him. There was too much doubt, or maybe not enough.

The room remained deathly quiet after he left. I could sense people staring at me, but I just kept methodically cutting my food and chewing it slowly. Minutes later when I looked up Lucinda was standing by my table, her face hard and inscrutable, her eyes small black ice chunks.

Her voice brittle, she said, "I liked you better when you were just an old coot."

"I'm sorry."

"Do me a favor and find some other place to eat breakfast. I'd just as soon never see you again."

"Lucinda, that was all a long time ago, I was a different person back then..."

My voice faded on me. The look on her face showed what I said didn't matter. "Okay, sure, if that's what you want." My voice again sounded distant and foreign to me. "As soon as I'm done here you won't see me again."

I turned away from her, fixed my attention back on my food and continued eating my breakfast. I would've liked a refill on my coffee, but I wasn't going to ask Lucinda for one, and instead planned on getting a cup at a convenience store. As I ate I looked up and met all of their stares until they looked away. I didn't care any more whether people recognized me. In a way this was good, it hardened me to the prospect. It also woke me up about the way I was spending money. I was living as if I only had another month or two left, but I'd already been out over a week without any sign of Lombard's boys, and the only relative of any of my victims who bothered looking me up turned out to be a gutless wonder who just wanted to spout off in front of an audience. It was possible that I was going to fade into the background, and that I'd be around a lot longer than I'd thought. I needed to quit eating out as much as I did, maybe buy a few pots and pans and start cooking more for myself.

The place was still as quiet as a tomb when I finished eating. I hesitated for a moment before dropping a twenty dollar bill to cover the food and tip, then left without looking back.

That afternoon I tried calling both Michael and Allison, and left them messages. I didn't expect them to return my calls, but maybe I'd wear them down over time. After that I went to the library, and a reference librarian helped me try to track down Paul's address and phone number on a computer. We came up empty. It was at best a wild goose chase. For all I knew he could've changed his last name, or be living overseas somewhere. He could even be dead for all I knew.

That same night while I was working I heard voices drifting in from the lobby. I was vacuuming a third-floor office when that happened. When I later asked the kid working security about it, he tried to look through me as if I didn't exist, then finally admitted that he had been talking to his girlfriend on the phone.

"Some sort of law against that?" he demanded.

"You better lose the attitude," I warned him, and left to finish my cleaning.

I thought about those voices I heard. It had sounded as if there was more than one person talking, but it was hard to tell with the noise the vacuum made, and by the time I'd realized what was happening and turned it off the conversation had ended. I guess it was possible the kid working security had his girlfriend on speakerphone, but that seemed far-fetched. More likely he was doing some business on the side, probably drugs, and had one or more customers over. If I was my old self I would've gotten the answer out of him quick enough, but I was no longer my old self. Besides, it was no concern of mine whether he was lying to me to cover some illegal activity. I had no interest in trying to push my way in on it, so it didn't really matter one way or the other.

I had more important things on my mind.

chapter 15

1978

Vincent DiGrassi's face looks older and grayer, as if he's aged five years in the six months since I've last seen him. He appears stiffer also. His neck and back must be bothering him with the way he's grimacing and the twisted off-kilter way he's holding himself. He gives me two names. One of them is Joey Lando.

"That one you got a history with," he acknowledges bluntly. "The same punk who sold you out to me after a five-minute beating."

So he remembers. Christ, that was thirteen years ago. The guy's mind is like a steel trap, nothing gets out of it. Even remembering every kid he ever ordered a beat-down on.

His grimace tightens, deep lines etch his face. "What the fuck the long face for?" he demands. "I thought you'd be chomping at the bit to pay that punk back."

"What's the reason for the hit?" I ask.

DiGrassi doesn't answer, just tries to stare me down, his grimace turning into something menacing.

"You're right," I say to break the silence. "I've got a history with him. You can tell me the reason for the hit."

The old DiGrassi would've been looking to tear my head off

for asking that. This one, there's something not quite right with him. His menacing look cracks, and he mutters something about Joey being a punk. "Is that good enough for you?" he asks sarcastically.

"I have my reasons for wanting to know," I say.

DiGrassi's eyes waver as he stares at me. He looks away first. "Your old rat friend is bringing special attention from the Feds because of his bank jobs. We asked him politely to lay off, and what does he do? The fucker hits five more deliveries to bank machines. And he doesn't even offer to kick over any of it. He's a punk, and a lesson needs to be made of him and his partner. Satisfied?"

"How come only two names?" I ask. "What about his inside person?"

DiGrassi's scowling at me. "What do you mean inside person?"

"The one working at the bank who's giving him the delivery schedules."

"How do you know this?"

"I just do."

At first his eyes blaze because I'm not giving him more of an explanation, but they slowly turn glassy as he calms down and accepts what I'm telling him. "Get this guy also."

"It's a woman."

"Whatever. And Lenny, make these bloody. The bodies have to be recognizable for the Feds, but this still has to be a statement."

It isn't hard finding Joey, nor is it hard getting him into the back of a stolen van. In his heart he believes I'm crooked and can't accept that I'm leading a clean life, so when I tell him I have forty cases of stolen booze that I want to unload cheap, he goes in willingly. Before he realizes what's happening, he's out cold.

I drive the van to a secluded garage where I have another stolen car waiting for me. Joey's tied up in back. It doesn't take much to get him to give up where his partner is holed up and the name of his inside person. No more than a couple of minutes of persuasion and only two lost fingernails. When I leave him he has this odd expression on his face, kind of a mix of hurt and validation.

I first go to Joey's apartment where I pick up enough evidence so I can tie him to the bank jobs, then I find his partner where he's holed up, and leave him sprawled out on the floor with a full clip from a forty-five in his torso. When I find their inside person I have a change of heart. She's just a wisp of a woman. Cute in her own way with stringy red hair and this innocent baby face that makes her look even younger than her twenty-four years. I've never killed a woman before – all my hits have been men, and I decide I don't want to start with this one. I end up making a deal with her instead. I have her type up a confession. I'm going to let her make a run for it. Maybe she makes it to Mexico before the Feds catch up to her, maybe she doesn't, but I let her know what will happen if she ever mentions a word about me. I'm wearing a ski mask so she can't identify me, and I show her Polaroids I took of Joey's partner so she knows I mean business. As far as DiGrassi is concerned, the story I'll give him is that someone must've tipped her off. He'll find the confession curious, but in the end he'll accept what I tell him. He has no reason to think that I'd go soft with a woman target. I watch as she packs a small suitcase and leaves. I'm not worried about her talking if she gets caught. If that happens, I'll deal with it.

When I return back to Joey, he's gotten himself a little more courage. Somehow he's convinced himself I'm just trying to rip him off. I listen to what he says, then I make it bloody like I'm supposed to. I leave behind the evidence tying him to the bank jobs. Then I leave the van in a place where it can be found after an anonymous tip.

I had put on overalls so I could finish the job with Joey without getting any blood splatters. I take them off, also an old pair of sneakers, and bring them with me so I can incinerate them later. I've also brought a change of clothes. The ones I'm wearing are clean but they'll be incinerated with the rest of the stuff. I know it's crazy, some sort of a phobia I've picked up, but I just don't want to risk my kids smelling death on me.

I slip on a pair of loafers that I brought along and I go to the YMCA so I can take a shower, change into my new clothes, and be clean for when I go home to Jenny and my two kids.

chapter 16

present

The next morning my cell phone rang again. I almost didn't answer it assuming it was the same tough guy from before, but then looked at the caller ID and saw it was my son, Michael. At first I didn't believe it, thinking my eyes were playing tricks on me.

"Michael?" I said, my voice cracking as I answered the phone.

"Yeah, it's me. You called yesterday." There was a pause, then, "I guess you're out of prison."

I laughed at that. I couldn't help it. "Come on, you must've seen something about it on the news."

"I don't watch much TV or read the papers these days. What do you want?"

"What do I want? Michael, I'm your father. Chrissakes, I haven't seen or heard from you in over fourteen years."

"You've got to be kidding me." There was another long pause before he added, "After what you did you're expecting some sort of father–son relationship? Are you out of your mind?"

His voice wasn't angry or sarcastic, just tired. I felt tongue-tied for a long moment before stumbling out with, "Whatever I did, it doesn't change that you're my son."

I'm sure it sounded as stupid and trite to him as it did to me. I sat cringing, waiting for his response. It seemed a long time before he answered me, and when he did his voice sounded like he was on the brink of exhaustion. Like it took every bit of strength he had to respond.

"Let me explain the obvious to you. You murdered twenty-eight people. For money. Whatever you were back then you were never my father. Fathers have real jobs, they're not mob hit men. They're not cold-blooded psychopaths. Do you have any idea what all that did to me? How many years of therapy I've gone through, and how fucked up I still am? And not just me, but Allie and Paul? And Mom, too. You don't think that had anything to do with her developing cancer?"

He wasn't telling me anything I hadn't thought about for years. After hearing about Jenny, I read everything I could about liver cancer in the prison library and I knew some people believed stress played a large role in it.

I said, "I just want to see you." I wanted to ask him for Paul's address and number, but stopped myself, knowing that that request would lead to a quick hang-up. Instead, carefully choosing my words, I added, "I don't want anything from you other than that. A half hour, Michael, that's all I'm asking."

"Yeah, well, you're asking a hell of a lot. I spoke to Allie this morning. She doesn't want you calling her again and leaving any more messages, so don't."

"Maybe Allie will change her mind someday."

"She's not changing her mind."

I hesitated, my voice lowering almost to a whisper. "Michael, you're my son. I love you. I just want to see you."

He laughed at that, a tired, exhausted laugh. "Next thing

you're going to tell me is that's what kept you surviving prison."

I lied then and told him it was partly that. In truth, I wasn't sure what it was that kept me going all those years. I knew it was self-preservation and anger that made me cut the deal in the first place. During those early years I was driven by wanting to see Jenny again, and to a lesser extent, wanting to walk out of prison as a big loud fuck-you to Lombard. After Jenny died and I no longer had any sort of life waiting for me on the outside, that fuck-you message I wanted to deliver stopped seeming all that important to me. I had to fight while inside prison to make it from day to day, but the thing was, I'd be damned if I knew why I bothered.

Michael took some time digesting what I told him. When he spoke again it was to tell me that I was lying, but there was a hint of doubt in his voice. "Don't call me again," he said. "Maybe I'll call you back someday, I'm not sure, but don't you ever fucking call me again."

He hung up then. I felt jittery inside, but also a little hopeful. Before his call, I never thought I would hear his voice again, and it went about as well as I could've expected.

Christ, my head was hurting me. Like it was being cracked open like a walnut. I sat for a while with my head bowed, cradling it in both hands. When I could I straightened up and reached for the bottle of aspirin that I kept next to the bed. My hand shook as I spilled several tablets into it. I chewed them slowly without bothering to get any water. I knew they weren't going to do much good. They never did much good.

Later that morning I was at a coffee shop trying to mind my own business while I ate a two dollar and fifty cent maple-banana-nut muffin and drank a three dollar cup of coffee – all of it costing more than a full breakfast at Lucinda's diner would've cost – when I noticed a woman sitting a few tables over staring at me. She was in her thirties, thick dark hair, dark features, probably of Italian descent, and all I could think was that I was about to have a confrontation with another of my victims' relatives.

I stared back. I didn't care. Let her shout and scream all she wanted. She got up from her table and walked over to me. Up close her hair was all tangled, like a hornet's nest. It looked like it hadn't been combed in days, that it needed washing and, even more badly, some work at a salon. But as bad a hair day as she might've been having it didn't hide that her features were striking, even given how skinny she was.

"I must've been staring," she said, keeping her voice soft and low. When I didn't say anything in response, she showed a trace of a shit-eating grin, and added, "I was there yesterday morning at the Blue Bell Diner when you and that fat guy gave us your two-man show. It was very entertaining. Do you mind if I join you?"

She waited a few seconds for me to answer her, and when I didn't, she sat across from me anyway, her shit-eating grin stretching a fraction of an inch. I remembered her then from the diner. She'd been sitting at a table in the back and I caught a glimpse of her when I stood up to leave. If she hadn't been so strikingly beautiful I wouldn't have noticed her. But as beautiful as she was, she was also somewhat a mess, both with her hair and her clothing, and no makeup on. My first thought would've been that she was a drug addict, except her eyes were bright and clear, and her skin too healthy for that.

"Did you follow me here?" I asked, my voice cracking and coming out as a hoarse rumble.

She laughed at that. It was a nice throaty laugh. "Hardly," she said. "Boy, are you one paranoid sonofabitch, but I guess given your situation I can't blame you for that." Her eyes glistened as she looked at me. "I was in here minding my own business when I recognized you from the other day. A coincidence, that's all."

"What do you want?"

She raised an eyebrow at that, her grin growing more amused. "It's not enough that a somewhat attractive woman wants to sit at the same table with you?" she asked.

Somewhat attractive didn't do her justice. Even as skinny and unkempt as she was, there was real beauty in her. Someone like her wasn't about to sit down at a table with a guy like me who was thirty years or so older than her, especially looking the way I did, unless she wanted something from me. After the stories broke about me six months ago I started receiving letters and photos from wack jobs who wanted to correspond with me in prison, a few even offering marriage proposals. Maybe it's a sadomasochism thing, maybe some bizarre attraction to death, or maybe just plain mental illness, but I discovered first hand that there are plenty of sickos out there who are attracted to serial killers, and I guess some of these looked on a professional hit man as being even more of a prize. Maybe this woman was one of them, except she didn't look it. With the prison letters I received, you could tell right away how insane these women were.

"Again, what do you want?"

Her lips pursing, she asked, "I have to want something?"

"Yeah."

"I'm not sure that's true," she said. Her eyes glistened several degrees brighter as she studied me. "What you went through in that diner yesterday was rough. I felt for you, but I also liked the way you handled yourself." She looked away for a moment, a solemnness momentarily weighing on her features. "I guess I also felt empathy. I've done plenty of things in the past that I'm not proud of, things that weren't so nice and that I wish

I could take back. I wouldn't be happy if complete strangers kept throwing them in my face. Fuck that guy yesterday, you know. From what you said, it sounds like you did the world a favor killing his scumbag rapist of an old man. Was what you said true? He really did that to that girl?"

I nodded.

"Well, good for you then."

"I don't have money stashed away, if that's what you're after."

More of that throaty laugh, her eyes shining again. "You don't trust people much, do you?"

"Not too much." I gave her a long hard look, trying to figure out what she was after. "I'm not killing anyone else, if that's what you're here for."

She didn't say anything in response to that, but the amusement in her eyes and smile showed that wasn't it either.

"You want to write a book about me, don't you?" I asked.

She shook her head and told me that she wasn't a writer, but there was a hesitation when she did so. So that was it. A wild stab in the dark, but I had figured her out. Another hopeful author who wanted to sell my life story for fame and fortune. At least this one was nice to look at, and more than that, had some personality. I felt comfortable with her.

She stood up, an impish smile still on her lips. She told me she had to get going, but that she lived in the area and she was sure she'd run into me now and again. She warned me if that happened for me not to get all paranoid and think she was following me. I had no doubt that I'd see her again. She'd make sure of it. She was smart enough where she'd give it some time before making her sales pitch about me writing a book with her, but I didn't much mind the prospect of that.

I watched as she walked away, noticing how nice her curves looked with her dressed in jeans and a tee shirt. Although she probably weighed no more than ninety pounds, I realized her build was more athletic and slender than skinny. Usually I liked a woman with more meat on her bones, but she was still stunning enough to stop your heart, especially with the way she smiled. It was almost a shame watching her slip on a bulky cotton jacket, but it didn't do much to hide how beautiful she was.

When she reached the door, she stopped to look back at me and give me a few more seconds of that shit-eating grin of hers. I almost called out to ask her her name, but I knew next time I saw her she would make sure to give it to me.

I felt an uneasiness after she left, and sat back and finished my muffin and coffee without really tasting much of either. When I was in prison I made sure to avoid other people and lived a mostly solitary existence. It wasn't safe otherwise, and the fight to stay alive and survive my stretch so I could someday walk out of prison gave me enough to focus on to make it easy. Now that I was out I found myself needing some sort of human interaction, and was looking forward to when I'd see this dark-haired beauty again, even if she was nothing but a con artist. And that was really what she was. Her plan was to befriend me, even hold out the promise of sex – not that there was any real chance of that happening – and eventually wear me down so I would agree to writing a book with her. I'd been around more than enough con men to know how this was going to work, but what she didn't understand was as much as she was trying to play a game on me, there actually was a connection between us. Not enough so that we'd ever end up romantically involved, but there was something there. Right now she was on too much of a high in working her game to get the book deal, but at some point she'd see it also.

My cell phone rang then. I stared at it, frowning, seeing that the caller ID was once again *unavailable*. I wasn't in the mood for a vague threat from some wannabe tough guy, so I turned off the phone instead of answering it. I was still stopping by the cell-phone store each day, but so far my salesman hadn't shown up again, and I was beginning to think he wasn't going to, that for some reason he must've quit his job.

I put the call out of my mind, and instead thought more about the woman who had just left me, and found myself anxiously looking forward to when I'd see her again. I knew it would be soon – she wouldn't let too much time go by, not with her just starting her game.

It turned out I was right. That Saturday I went to the same coffee shop and she was already camped out there with a dog-eared paperback in one hand and a large cup of coffee in the other. I'd done the same plenty of times when I was waiting for a target.

She glanced up shortly after I'd walked into the shop, and as she saw me her eyes grew exaggeratedly large. With a wicked grin, she accused me of stalking her. I shook my head, but that grin of hers was infectious enough to crack a smile from me, which doesn't happen often. She waited until after I bought a coffee and slice of lemon pound cake and had been sitting alone for a few minutes before getting up from her table and asking if she could join me.

"It looks like you could use the company," she said, her grin even more wicked.

"Yes, sure, I'd like that."

I felt a pang of guilt knowing that I wasn't going to be agreeing to write a book with her. I should've told her point blank there wasn't any chance of it happening and let her drop her game, but I couldn't. Like the other day, she was strikingly beautiful, but also unkempt. Her hair was the same tangled hornet's nest and her clothes were badly worn and tattered. She probably bought them from a similar thrift store to the one I had shopped at earlier, except in her case she had worn them to near threads. She was clearly in the midst of a bad stretch, and had latched on to this book idea as a way to pull herself out. As beautiful as she was she could've made a nice income as a stripper, and an even nicer one as a high-class hooker, but I guess no matter how hard up she was for money she wasn't about to resort to either of those, and that just made me like her all the more.

She took the seat across from me and showed me the paperback she had been reading, *The Godfather* by Mario Puzo. "I bought it for twenty-five cents at a garage sale," she told me. Either she was doing research or she was trying to send me some sort of subtle message that I wasn't getting.

"What do you do for work?" I asked.

"Wow, a bit abrupt, aren't we?" she said, her voice light, amused. "But to answer your question, a little bit of this and that, but right now I'm in between jobs." Her eyes lowered as she took a sip of her coffee. When she looked up and met my eyes again, her smile had turned wistful. "I'd heard about you in the news before, but really didn't pay much attention. After we met the other day, I went to the library and dug up some of the stories about you. I was so sorry to read that your wife died while you were in prison. That must've been hard."

I nodded, didn't say anything.

"Those people you killed, let me guess, they weren't quite as innocent and pure as the driven snow as the papers made them out to be?"

"No, they weren't," I said with only a slight hesitation. The two men I had killed with Behrle turned out to be friends of his, and they both turned out to be even worse scumbags than he ever was. I had looked into it after the hit, and they were involved in a string of home invasions, one of which left a teenage girl paralyzed. I had no remorse for those two.

"Fucking newspapers," she said. "They can make the worst scum out to be a fucking saint." A hardness momentarily tightened her smile, and I had this sense about her then that she had blood on her hands also. Maybe an abusive partner, maybe some incestuous relative. I wouldn't have been surprised if she had done a stretch in prison too, but I didn't ask her about any of that.

She was still absorbed in her thoughts, and had absently pulled a pack of Newports from her jacket pocket. She tapped a cigarette out, slid it in her mouth, and was about to light up before she remembered where she was.

"Think they'd throw me in jail if I lit up in here?" she asked, the cig now out of her mouth and held lightly between her index and middle fingers.

"No doubt," I said.

Her gaze wandered past me, and she stuck out her tongue at a coffee shop employee who had been glaring openly at her. Smiling to herself, she put the cig behind her ear.

"I need this badly right now," she told me, referring to the cig. She gestured with her eyes that I was welcome to join her outside while she lit up, but I stayed in my seat. She opened her eyes wider in mock surprise over the fact that I wasn't jumping at the chance to join her, and before she turned to leave, told me she was sure we'd bump into each other again. I was sure of that also.

I was a little surprised she hadn't given me her name yet. I would've thought that would've happened after our second "chance" meeting. It turned out she didn't disappoint me. She was halfway to the door when she turned on her heels and walked back to my table, offering me her hand.

"By the way, my name's Sophie Duval," she said.

"Leonard March," I said.

"As if you're telling me something I don't already know," she said with a wink. I watched the way her slender hips moved as she headed back to the front door. Christ, she was gorgeous. At least thirty years younger than me and absolutely gorgeous. When she reached the door, she stopped to snap off a quick army-type salute in my direction, then left. I wondered briefly when I'd be bumping into her again. I knew it wouldn't be long.

It was Tuesday when I saw her next. At around seven-thirty in the evening I was walking along Moody Street to my job when I heard footsteps racing behind me. Next thing I knew an arm was hooking mine and a small hand resting on my leather jacket sleeve below the elbow. It was Sophie. Her face was flushed. In a breathless whisper she told me that it looked like a car was following me.

It was a cold late October night with the wind whipping up, and I'd been walking with my head bowed and hadn't been paying much attention to the street. I turned and saw that she was right. A light blue Chevrolet sedan was creeping along keeping pace with me. There were two men in the car. Both looked hardened. The driver slid his glance sideways and noticed me looking his way. His eyes were cold and empty, his face scarred and with a toughness to it. Without any change of expression, he stared straight ahead and sped away.

Sophie recited some random numbers. I stared at her, confused.

"The license plate," she said. "Damn, Leonard, you have to pay more attention to what's going on around you. There are obviously people out there holding grudges."

"I was hoping I had already slipped into yesterday's news."

"Obviously not." Her face had flushed to a deep red. There

was so much excitement in her eyes. "You know, I might've saved your life tonight. I might have to think of a way for you to repay me."

It was possible she was right. Those two in the blue Chevrolet could've been Lombard's boys. They had the look of it. But it could also be part of the game Sophie was running. An awful big coincidence her being there at the right time to warn me about that car, but not if she had arranged it in the first place.

"Any idea how I'll be able to do that?" I asked.

"I'll think of something."

I had thrown it out there, and she decided to play me the right way and not be too anxious for her pitch. If she had asked me then about writing a book with her, she'd be tipping her hand that it was all a con and that she already had her payoff in mind. I wondered which it was with that car. It could just as likely have been Lombard's boys as an arrangement by Sophie, but the more I thought about it the more I was leaning towards Lombard. Sophie probably knew my routine by now, and was most likely out there looking for me when she happened to see me and the car, then realized quickly how she could use it.

We walked another two blocks without either of us saying a word. The feel of her hand on my arm and the occasional touch of her hip against mine damn near took my breath away, and she knew the effect she was having on me. We were a block away from the side street I needed to take for my job when she told me that this was where she was getting off and that she'd see me around. She let go of my arm and I watched mesmerized as she walked into a small Hispanic grocery store. For a few seconds all I could think of was the feel of her hand on my arm. After the door had closed behind her and she was out of sight, I felt a heavy sigh rumble out of me, and I trudged off to work.

Chapter 17

1979

Vincent DiGrassi opens an eye as I approach him. He's lying propped up on his bed. Both his eyes are now open. As yellowish and bloody as they are, there's still an alertness to them. He knows full well why I'm there. I pull a chair up next to him and sit so I'm resting the forty-five and its attached silencer on my thigh. What used to be such a robust bull of a man is now only skin and bones. He's probably dropped eighty pounds in the past year.

"Sal send you?" he asks, his voice not much more than a croak.

"Yeah."

He digests that, puckers up his mouth, and says in an aggrieved tone, "So you're dealing with Sal directly now."

"Yeah, ever since it's been clear how sick you are."

The little that's left of his face folds into an ugly frown. At first I think he's going to start bawling, but he turns his eyes towards me and stares with utter fury.

"This is bullshit," he insists.

I shrug. What is there for me to say?

"I'm not talking to no cops. There's no reason for Sal wanting this."

I scratch behind an ear, smile at him sadly. "What if you end up hopped up on drugs? Who knows what you say then. Vincent, you know this has to be done."

"You little punk, you calling me Vincent now? What the fuck happened to Mr DiGrassi?"

I don't say anything. His color's not much better than gray now. He looks away, the fury fades from his eyes leaving them glassy.

"You can tell Sal I'm not going to any hospital," he says. "I plan on dying in my own bed."

My smile grows more genuine thinking how right he is. I realize this and force a somber look. "Your wife or kids might think differently. Mr Lombard can't take the chance. You have to know that."

"Don't you fucking patronize me," he spits out. Then, showing his self pity, he adds, "Fuck you. After everything I've done for you."

"I'm sorry."

His eyes slide sideways to look at me. "That business last year with that skirt you were supposed to hit. The one you claimed was tipped off and made a run for it."

He was referring to Joey Lando's inside person. The one I let get away. "Yeah, what about it?" I say.

"Sal and some of his boys thought it sounded funny. They thought maybe you'd gone soft and couldn't hit a skirt. I went out on a limb for you and convinced them you were on the level. I hadn't done that you'd be buried in a landfill now."

He's staring hard at me, trying to read inside me. He sees what he's looking for and turns away. "What the fuck do you know," he mutters. "They were right."

His thick lips curl to show the contempt he feels for me.

"She was just a kid," I explain. "It wouldn't have been right."

"Who the fuck are you to make that decision? A bank guard died in those robberies your rat punk buddy did and she was as responsible as the other two of them."

He realizes then the irony in chastising me for being sentimental and not killing one of my targets while at the same time trying to talk me into doing the same now. I can see the confusion clouding up his eyes.

"You don't have to use the forty-five," he says after a while. "You can use the pillow instead. That way Angie and my kids can have an open casket."

He's bracing himself waiting. I don't move. There's been something I've been wanting to ask him for a long time.

"That hit I did right before my wedding. Who the fuck was that guy?"

His eyes come alive once he remembers the hit. He starts laughing. It's a weak, broken-down type laugh, and before too long he starts choking on it, then breaks into a coughing fit. After he settles down, he nods and tells me, "You."

I'm confused. I ask him what he means.

"The guy you hit was the same as you. Another hit man for Sal."

"Why'd I hit him?"

DiGrassi makes a face showing his disgust. "'Cause he got soft. Claimed one of his targets skipped town to parts unknown without him tipping the target off. Sal didn't believe him. Neither did I. So are you going to use the fucking pillow or what?"

I shake my head, push the barrel of the forty-five against his right temple. He's too weak to put up any fight.

"I'm sorry, Mr DiGrassi," I say. "But I have to do it the way Mr Lombard told me to do it."

"Motherfucker," he starts, "you owe me at least a call to Sal to ask him—"

Before DiGrassi can finish the sentence I pull the trigger and send a good chunk of his brain splattering against the wall. Then I shove the barrel into his dead mouth and shoot off three more rounds. Sal wants his boys to think DiGrassi was a rat. That's the reason for the violent death. It's easier to explain the hit of a loyal friend that way. Who knows, maybe we get lucky and the cops think that a rival did the job.

I use the sheet to wipe the blood off the gun. I give DiGrassi's lifeless body one last look before leaving. He should've been grateful to me for taking him out of his misery the way I did instead of all his bitching and moaning, but I don't want to let a last few minutes color my memory of him. Jenny's pregnant with our third kid. She's convinced it's going to be a boy. I play around with the thought of Vincent March for a name, but decide against it.

DiGrassi's wife and kids are out of the house, which makes things easier for me. With the house empty, I think about taking a shower to clean the smell of death off me, but I decide that can wait until I go to the YMCA. Besides, they have a steam room there. I let myself out the back door, same way I came in.

chapter 18

present

It was the next day when I spotted two punks working themselves up to rob a liquor store. At the time I was walking to the library and they were standing across the street, both in their early twenties, their heads shaved and their bodies thin to the point of emaciated. They were dressed the same, wearing loose-fitting khaki pants and the type of faded dungaree jackets that you used to be able to buy at army surplus stores. The one that I could see more clearly looked like he was having a tough time standing still, his face folded into a scowl and his eyes fixed in a death stare. I'd been around enough crystal meth users in prison to see immediately that these two were on the stuff. In my younger days I'd also robbed enough stores to know what they were planning even without seeing the bulge a gun made tucked inside one of their waistbands. I knew even before I saw them pull their ski masks out.

I wanted to keep walking. The last thing I wanted to do was get involved, but I stopped in my tracks, paralyzed. I could see how wired these two punks were, and all I could imagine was how trigger-happy they were going to be once inside the liquor store. The people they were going to kill in there would be more blood on my hands. Reluctantly, I found myself jogging across the street, then tapping the one with the gun on the shoulder and asking him if he had a smoke.

He turned to face me, his ski mask pulled on three quarters of the way. His eyes empty as he faced me, his exposed mouth ugly and his body twitching.

"What the fuck you want?" he demanded, his voice just as tight and wired as I had imagined.

"You got a cigarette?" I asked again.

"Yeah, I got something for you to suck on, you stupid fuck."

He was taking the .38 from his waistband. There was no doubt from the violence shining in his eyes that he was planning to shoot me. I stepped in quickly, and with my left hand took the gun away from him while at the same time hitting him in the throat with my right. The punch left him making funny noises as he struggled to breathe. Without giving him a chance to recover, I sent him hard on his ass on the concrete sidewalk, then kicked him in the head hard enough to bounce it off the concrete and put him out.

His buddy turned around then. He was still pulling his ski mask on, and I could see the dazed look in his eyes as he first stared at me and then his buddy on the ground. Slowly comprehension worked its way in.

"You dumb motherfucker," he near spat at me.

It turned out he also had a gun in his waistband, but he was too hyped up to see that I was holding a .38 on him. He started to pull his weapon out. I could've blown him to hell, but instead I flipped the .38 in my hand and rapped him in the jaw with the gun butt. The blow sent him to his knees and his own gun tumbling out of his hand. I picked it up and dropped it in my jacket pocket. He looked up at me, blood coming out pretty good from his mouth, a thick purple bruise already showing on his jaw. His eyes were big as he noticed for the first time that I was holding a .38 on him. One of his pupils looked dilated, showing that he had concussion. A little known fact: a blow to the jaw can cause a concussion.

"Get on your stomach," I ordered.

"Hey, man, you don't have to do this."

I gestured with the gun that he'd better listen to me.

"If you quit acting like a dumb fuck, we can give you a cut," he said.

It was laughable. His buddy out cold, him bleeding and with concussion, and he was still thinking of robbing the liquor store. I shook my head at him, and something about my expression made him listen to me and get down on his stomach.

A couple of people came out of the liquor store curious about the commotion. Their faces blanched when they saw the two punks bleeding as they lay on the sidewalk, and me holding a gun on them.

"Can someone please call the police?" I asked them.

Somebody already had. The next moment I heard the sirens approaching, then tires screeching. Without turning to look I knew that two cruisers had pulled to a stop behind me. I didn't want them coming out with their weapons drawn and me holding a gun on these two. I lowered the gun I was holding and placed it by my feet, then raised my hands so they were visible. The punk on his stomach watched this, and I caught the calculating look in his eyes as he tried to decide whether it was worth making a run for it, or maybe even a dive for the gun. I heard the doors to the police cruisers being thrown open, then one of the cops yelling for nobody to move.

"Officer, I have another gun in my jacket pocket," I yelled to them. "I took both guns off these two meth heads right before they were about to rob this liquor store."

"That old man's a psycho," the punk on his stomach tried arguing, his voice barely a rasp. "We weren't going to rob nothing, and I ain't on any meth. This psycho attacked me and my brother for nothing. And those guns are his. I never saw them before."

Maybe what he was saying would've carried more weight if he and his brother weren't wearing ski masks. I glanced over my shoulder and saw one of the cops giving the punk a glazed-eyed stare. This cop noticed me looking at him and told me to stand where I was, then walked over to me so he could take the gun from my jacket pocket and pick up the one by my feet.

"Any of you see what happened?" this cop asked the bystanders. He was a good ten years younger than me, but still looked older than the other cops at the scene, with gray hair cut close to the scalp and a fatigued expression on his long face. He reminded me of an older version of Roy Scheider from *The French Connection*.

The bystanders shook their heads in response to his question. One of them told him that they came out of the store after they heard a fight outside, but didn't see anything except me holding a gun on the two youths.

This older cop let out a tired sigh. He told me I could lower my hands, and asked me to tell him how I knew these two were planning on robbing the store. The would-be robber lying on his stomach tried arguing that they weren't planning on robbing anyone. Another cop who was in the process of handcuffing him pushed his face into the sidewalk to shut him up.

"The two of them looked suspicious standing outside the liquor store," I told the older cop. "When I saw a gun sticking out of that one's waistband" – I nodded towards the one who was out cold – "and then saw them both putting on ski masks, I knew what they were going to do, and knew that if I didn't stop them, as hyped up as they were acting, they were going to be killing people in there."

The cop I was telling this to stared at me incredulously. "What did you do to stop them?" he asked. I told him and his incredulity only intensified. He looked as if I were telling him a joke and he was waiting for the punchline. One of the other cops recognized me then. I could see it in the shift in his expression. He pulled this older cop aside and said something to him. I was warned then to make sure to keep my hands visible, and I watched as the cop I'd been talking to went back to his squad car and got on his two-way. When he came back his attitude towards me had changed.

"Put your hands behind your back," he told me.

"What for?"

"We need to bring all of you in and sort this out," he said.

I caught the rapt attention on the punk's face. Concussion or not, he knew something was up, and he was trying to figure out what it was. I looked back at the older cop in front of me, the one who wanted to handcuff me. His eyes wavered as I met his stare, and I could see some worry there. I was sure he dealt with more than his share of violent crime, but it was probably domestic stuff or kids acting stupid. I was different; a hit man with twenty-eight kills, and someone who had been all over the news for months. He wasn't quite sure how to deal with someone like me.

"What's there to sort out?" I asked him. "What the fuck do you think went on here with these two meth heads wearing ski masks and carrying guns?"

"We took the guns off you, not them," he said stiffly. "And until we sort this out the only crimes we have evidence of so far are assault and battery committed by you, and possession of unlicensed firearms, also committed by you. Now put your hands behind your back. I'm not telling you again."

There was still a lot of worry in his eyes. The other cops with him edged closer to me. I put my hands behind my back and felt a throbbing pain in my right shoulder. I must've hurt it earlier and didn't realize it until now because of the adrenaline rush. I told the cop about the pain in my shoulder and asked him if I could be cuffed in front instead. He ignored me and cuffed me behind. The punk who had been on his stomach was pulled up to his feet. He smirked at me. He had no idea what was going on but he knew something was working in his favor.

While I was being put in the back seat of a squad car, an ambulance pulled up to the scene. The guy I had knocked out cold was mostly still out, and they were loading him on to a stretcher. I watched all this until the squad car I was in drove off.

At the precinct, I was brought to an interrogation room, and only then were the handcuffs taken off. They took my cell phone from me, and I was left alone for an hour until a Detective John Fallow came in. He was in his forties, balding, pasty complexion, and in his cheap suit looked more like an accountant than a cop. I told him about my shoulder hurting. He ignored me and told me we needed to clear up what happened at the liquor store, and he had me go over my account of what happened.

"Here's the problem we have," he said. "One of the men you accosted, Jason Mueller, has given us a completely different version of the events. The other man, his brother, Thomas Mueller, has only recently regained consciousness and is receiving medical attention, but we'll get his version soon."

"Did Jason tell you why he and his brother were wearing ski masks on a day when it was over sixty degrees out?" I asked.

"Yes, as a matter of fact he did." Fallow offered me a grim smile. "He claims you tried forcing them into committing armed robbery. That you made them put the ski masks on, but that when they refused to rob the liquor store you beat them both up."

He had said that with a straight face. All I could do was stare at him and wonder where this was coming from; whether someone in the District Attorney's office thought they could use this to send me back to prison, or whether they believed that punk's story. Or maybe it was a matter of them wanting badly to believe his story.

Fallow and me kept up our staring contest; him offering his grim, polite smile, me trying hard to keep my temper in check.

"This is ridiculous," I finally said, breaking the silence in the room. "If you check their arrest records, I'll bet they're lengthy and with other armed robberies."

"Possibly," he admitted, "but I doubt they're as lengthy as your own."

"You've got a bet," I told him. "I was only arrested once."

He smiled at that. I could see the argument forming that all the crimes I admitted to would be a far longer list than their arrest records could possibly be. Instead, he asked why I would've wanted to stop them from robbing the liquor store.

"I don't understand what you're asking," I said, genuinely confused.

His smile turned patronizing. "If what you're telling us is true, that you saw the two men standing outside a liquor store and you knew they were about to rob it, why would you get involved? I'm sorry, Mr March, but from what I've read about you, that doesn't make sense."

"How am I supposed to answer that?" I asked. "Are you saying that I'm incapable of doing something decent?"

He scratched the back of his head as he thought about that. "Yes, I guess that's exactly what I'm saying. It's not believable, Mr March, that you'd stick your neck out the way you did, nor is it believable that a man of your age and slight build could disable and overpower two armed men in their twenties, especially, as you claim, two men hopped up on crystal meth."

"What's hard to believe is you accepting this meth head's story. Have you tested these two punks for drugs?"

He didn't answer me. Just kept smiling his polite, grim smile. I took a deep breath and fought a losing battle with my anger.

"Why would I have two guns with me?" I heard myself asking him. "What the fuck was I doing with them, trying to force those two punks to take them off me to commit an armed robbery? Then what happened, they refused and I beat them up? Christ, use some fucking brains. If any of that were true – if they were such innocents – why wouldn't they take the guns from me and hold me until the police arrived? Talk about your shitbrained fairy tales. You really think there's a chance the other brother will tell the same story, at least if he isn't prepped?"

"You have quite a temper, don't you, Mr March?"

I closed my mouth. I understood then that he was only trying to get a rise out of me, trying to get me to say something that could be used later against me. It wasn't worth saying another word to him.

He waited patiently, and only when he realized I wasn't going to answer him, he continued, "To answer your question, I don't fully believe Jason Mueller's story, just as I don't believe yours. The truth most likely lies somewhere in the middle. If I had to guess, you recruited these two brothers for the liquor store robbery, then had some sort of falling out with them at the last minute and things turned violent between you. But if that's the case, we're never going to find that out, and given your extremely violent past, their version of the events has to be considered more credible. While it would be nice to lock all three of you away, I'll settle for sending you back to prison, Mr March. Or should I call you Leonard?"

I saw the way it was going to be then. If the other brother, the one I knocked out cold, had any smarts, he would claim a temporary loss of memory rather than risk contradicting his brother's story. As insane as it was, I could very well end up going back to prison for the one decent thing I did in my life – and they'd send me for the maximum sentence they could. I should've gotten a good laugh out of the whole thing, but instead I felt sick to my stomach thinking how this was going to be played up in the papers and how justified my kids were going to feel in writing me off for good. I felt even sicker knowing that I would never see Sophie Duval again. Absently, I started massaging my throbbing shoulder while Fallow stared at me as if I were some sort of bug that he had pinned down under a magnifying glass.

There was a knock on the outside door. Fallow looked away from me, annoyed. He got up and had a quick conversation with whoever it was outside the door, then left me alone. While I sat in the room, I slipped into despair. It didn't make much sense for me to feel that way. It wasn't as if I had that much going for me on the outside; a few more chance encounters with Sophie before she would bring up her book idea and I would turn her down, the slim hope that my kids would give me a break and meet with me. That was really about all I had, but the thought of losing it still sent me sinking into utter blackness.

I don't know how long I was alone. Maybe a half hour, maybe longer, but when the door opened again a different cop walked in. This one was bulkier with a face like a bulldog's, his hair silver, his suit more expensive. He looked uncomfortable as he cleared his throat and introduced himself as Captain Edmund Gormer.

"I would like to apologize for any inconvenience that has been caused you," he muttered in a rumbling voice. He looked past me, unable to meet my eyes, his voice sounding as if he hated every second of what he was doing. "We had to clear up a confusing situation, but that has been done, and as captain of this precinct I would like to thank you for doing your civic duty today, both in thwarting a felony and in apprehending two dangerous criminals. I believe these are yours."

He handed me my wallet and cell phone. So either the other brother was stupid enough to give a statement instead of claiming a loss of memory, or a witness had come forward to corroborate my version of the story. I kept a stoical exterior. I wasn't going to show this cop shit.

"What about the bottle of aspirin your cops took off me?" I asked. "That Roy Scheider lookalike patrolman of yours injured my shoulder when he handcuffed me behind my back. I need those aspirin."

His skin color was a muddled gray as he told me he'd find out where my aspirin was. He cleared his throat again, and with a false smile that badly contradicted the glumness in his eyes, he told me there was going to be a press conference soon at which they were going to explain my heroism to the media. "We would like you to be there to answer their questions," he added half-heartedly.

I shook my head. "I just want to get my aspirin and get the hell out of here." While I told him this I had looked through my wallet. I stared up at him and told him a hundred and fifty dollars was missing. "Fuck it, maybe I will speak to the media after all," I said.

Alarm showed in his eyes. "I'll look into this," he said. "Please wait here."

Nothing had been taken out of my wallet, but I figured a hundred and fifty was more than a fair price for the ordeal they had put me through. Less than ten minutes later Captain Gormer returned handing me a new bottle of aspirin and a hundred and fifty dollars. All I could imagine was them sending out a squad car with the siren on to buy me the aspirin. I opened the bottle with my left hand, dumped a couple of tablets into my mouth, then asked Gormer whether the media was camped outside. He told me they were.

"Is there a back way out of here?" I asked.

He nodded, relief in his eyes. "I'll have a patrolman show you the way," he said.

I should've asked Gormer how they were able to corroborate my statement. I had assumed it was either Thomas Mueller fucking things up for him and his brother or a witness coming forward. It turned out it was something else entirely, and it creeped me out when I saw what it was.

I was sitting in a bar having a few Michelob drafts and trying to get my nerves under control when the news came on and a video was played that had been sent to them anonymously earlier in the day. The video showed it all; from when I stopped to watch the Mueller brothers outside the liquor store, to me running across the street and everything that followed until the police showed up. It would've been impossible for the police to have twisted that video to support Jason Mueller's statement, and I should've been grateful that that video existed, but I couldn't help feeling a queasiness in my gut realizing that someone had been following me without me realizing it. Not only following me, but videoing me.

Several of the other bar patrons had started staring at me as they recognized me from the video. When they showed my prison photo and talked about my recent release from prison and my violent history, more eyes turned my way. After the photo, they cut to a press conference where Captain Gormer talked about my heroism, all the while looking like he had a tooth that needed pulling. The bar became deathly quiet, the only sound coming from the TV set. No one spoke a word to me. The bartender stood off to the side looking increasingly uncomfortable as he tried to catch glimpses of me without meeting my eye. I sat silently drinking my draft, the tips of my ears burning hot. When I finished I got up and left, feeling all eyes in the bar following me out the door.

While I walked back to my apartment, more heads turned my way. This was what I didn't want. I had started to fade from the news and become invisible, and now I was being put right back on the front page. Knowing that that would happen had frozen me earlier and almost had me turning a blind eye away from the two punks gearing themselves up outside the liquor store. As awkward as it was watching the news in that bar, it was also interesting seeing the confusion on the anchor's face as she struggled with knocking my horns off and putting a halo on me. All in all, though, it left me unsettled.

I stopped off at a convenience store for a bag of ice. I wasn't sure if it would do any good, but I thought I'd use the ice for my shoulder. When I got to my apartment door and saw the match I had forced between the door and the doorjamb lying on the floor, I knew someone had been inside. The lock hadn't been tampered with, so that person had either been given a key or was good with locks. I went into the apartment and saw pretty quickly that the place had been searched. It wouldn't have been obvious to the average person since clothes hadn't been tossed on the floor and nothing appeared out of place, but to me it was as plain as day. I had done things to let me know if drawers had been opened or items moved. I made a quick search to see if anything was missing, and found that the money I had taped on the inside of the radiator cover was still there. After dusting myself off and chewing on a few aspirin, I went to the apartment building's administrative office.

The same dull heavy woman from before was working, or at least she was supposed to be. She offered me an empty fish-eyed stare before turning back to the magazine she was reading.

"Someone was inside my apartment," I said.

"Apartments were sprayed today for pests," she said flatly and without looking at me. "Notices were sent last week."

"I didn't get a notice."

"You should have."

She went back to reading her magazine. I watched for a minute before telling her that I wanted the name of the pest-control service they used. "Whoever it was, they searched my apartment," I added.

She put down her magazine and turned her fish-eyed stare back at me. "How do you know this? Your place trashed?"

"No, but whoever did this went through my drawers."

"Anything missing?"

"No, nothing's missing."

"Then what's your beef?" she asked, challenging me more with that ugly fish-eyed stare.

"Are you sure it wasn't the police in my apartment?"

"I told you who it was."

I couldn't read whether she was lying or not. "Did someone pay you to get inside my apartment?" I asked.

Her mouth tightened as she stared at me. "I've had enough of your nonsense," she said, her voice still flat and dull. "You don't like our policies here, find yourself another address. Now get out of my office before I call the police."

There was no point in trying to get anything out of her, at least not by talking, and I wasn't about to resort to my old methods. I left her and went back to my apartment where I first looked around the kitchen for any chemicals that a pest-control person would've left, then put some ice in a plastic bag, sat down in my recliner and held the ice against my right shoulder. If a pest-control person had been in there, I couldn't find any sign of chemicals being sprayed in the kitchen, nor could I smell much beyond the damp mildewy odor that my apartment always had.

When I showed up at work later the kid working security gave me the same sort of confused look that that TV anchor had showed earlier. "I saw that video," he said.

This was the first time he had willingly spoken to me, and it stopped me. "Yeah?" I said. "You caught me on the news?"

He shook his head. "No, YouTube."

I didn't know what that was, but I felt some sort of encouragement that he was volunteering to have a conversation with me. More just to keep it going than out of any real curiosity, I asked him what he thought.

He handed me the office keys and had me sign the checkout sheet before telling me that I must've had some sort of angle for doing what I did. "You're no hero, that's for damn sure," he said, his eyes hard as they met mine.

"Fuck you," I told him, and I left him to go do my job.

I started off the night listening to music, but after twenty minutes or so curiosity got the better of me and I tuned into the same talk show that had been talking about me when I first got out of prison. They were talking about me again; this time the calls were all over the place with some callers claiming that what I did didn't change the fact that I was a murderous scumbag and a rat to boot and that I was still going to get mine in the end, others thinking I had some ulterior motive for my heroism, while a few scattered callers talked about forgiveness and redemption and how I should be given credit for potentially saving lives inside that liquor store. I didn't much enjoy listening to any of it, but I couldn't turn it off, and after a while I admitted to myself the reason why – that I was hoping that Allison, or at least the woman who sounded like my daughter, would call back in. She didn't.

The talk show discussed me for two hours before they moved on to a different topic. I went through the radio dial then, but couldn't find any other shows talking about me. I turned the radio off, not much in the mood to listen to anything. As it was, because of my shoulder I was moving slower than usual and was behind schedule. I had been chewing aspirin all night, but it didn't help much, and I was only able to lift my right arm up to my chest. When I tried lifting it higher, the pain brought tears to my eyes. I tried pushing myself harder to catch up, but I didn't finish cleaning the last office until two-thirty. When I checked the keys back in the kid working security made a comment about me being late.

"So what?"

"You're supposed to finish by two o'clock," he said peevishly. "Not spending a half-hour extra in those offices taking a nap or whatever else you were doing. That's so what. I'll have to report this."

His new-found boldness was annoying and I decided I liked it better when he was too afraid to say much of anything. I leaned in closer to him and told him how he looked like a guy I once knew, and it was the truth.

"Duane Halvin," I said. "Big roly-poly kid. Thirty years old and still had baby fat. Christ, the two of you could've been separated at birth." I leaned in closer, added, "I had to put an ice pick through his eye, and the thing was, I used to see Duane all the time at the track and I liked the guy. He was fun to hang around. You, not so much."

His hard grin fell slack once he registered what I was saying. I left him then, remembering how the same pretty much happened with Duane Halvin once he realized what I had the ice pick for.

I've never been a heavy drinker, usually limiting myself to a couple of beers or a shot now and again. When I got back to my apartment I poured six ounces of cheap whiskey into a glass. With how anxious I was, and with the way my mind was racing and my shoulder throbbing like hell, I knew without the whiskey I'd have no chance of sleeping. After I drank it, I sat in my recliner and held a bag of ice to my shoulder, waiting until my eyelids felt heavy before moving to the bed.

Mercifully, I was out after I closed my eyes.

chapter 19

1980

My mom's waiting by the curb. While we talk on the phone every week for about a minute, this is the first time I've seen her in three years, even though we live only twenty minutes from each other. Our weekly conversation always goes the same way:

"How are you, mom?"

"Fine. And yourself?"

"Fine."

"That's good. Your children?"

"Fine."

"Well, goodbye then."

She never asks about Jenny, which is expected since the two of them don't get along, to put it mildly. As far as I go, our weekly conversations are on a par with any we've ever had. Our relationship has always been an uneasy truce. I don't think there was ever a time we felt comfortable together, and while she never said as much in words, she made it clear in actions and attitude that I should've been the son to die early, not my brothers, Tony and Jim.

She looks the same since I've seen her last. Plump, sturdy frame, gray hair in a bun and as tightly wound as steel wool. Her face round and placid, her legs like small tree stumps. The black dress she's wearing is hanging off her like a canvas sack. If she were living in a remote village near some forest in Russia, she'd look like the type of woman who could out-wrestle a wolf if she had to and make Sunday dinner out of it. In her wedding pictures she was beautiful. Slender, narrow, heart-shaped face, thick black hair that fell past delicate bare shoulders. Hard to believe it's the same person. I don't know when she changed. Outside of her gray hair, I can't remember her ever looking much different than she does now.

I pull the car up next to her. She gets in, and up close I notice how much older she actually looks, her skin more faded and wrinkled, her eyes duller. Still, her face is locked in a dour frown, almost as if it's been carved out of stone. She asks where her grandchildren are.

"They're too young for this," I say.

"I was hoping to see them," she says, her German-Jewish accent as thick as ever.

"Some other time."

We both know it won't be any time soon. How many times have we seen each other in the last ten years? Three times is all I can remember, and I think we both prefer it this way. There's a discomfort between us. I can feel it in my gut, and even though she's sitting stoically with her hands folded in her lap, I know she feels it too. It's funny how I always felt so at ease with my pop, and never with her.

As I'm pulling the car away from the curb I tell her she didn't have to wait for me outside, that she could've waited inside her apartment and I would've come and got her. She only hesitates for a second before telling me that she didn't want me to have to find a parking space, especially given how difficult it can be finding free parking around there. It's a bald-faced lie. There are a half dozen empty spots in plain view. We both know the reason is because she doesn't want me in her apartment, and she certainly doesn't want to have to explain me to any of her friends or neighbors we might bump into. As far as she's concerned her two sons are dead, and I've always been something else entirely.

We drive in silence to the cemetery with neither of us bothering to make small talk. I notice her looking at the Rolex watch Sal Lombard gave me. It was stupid of me wearing it, not that it much matters. I could give her some bullshit explanation about winning it in a poker game or having a good week at the track, but she'll know I'm lying. She has no reason to think that I do anything other than work in a liquor store, but it's always been like she knows I make my money other ways than the job I'm supposed to have. I don't bother explaining the Rolex to her, there's no point.

On the way to the cemetery I stop off to buy flowers. While I do this, my mom sits silently in the car. When I return I hand her the dozen white roses I bought. Her mouth crumbles for a moment before she gets her emotion under control.

"What about for your brothers," she says. "You can't be bothered to buy flowers for them?"

We're going to the cemetery for the twentieth anniversary of my pop's death. If she wanted me to buy flowers for Tony and Jim she should've said something instead of stewing in all her regret. I feel a vein pulsing along my temple, and I swallow back what I want to say, instead tell her that we can split the roses among all three graves. I know she's not happy with that, but I'm not about to go back into that store because of some fucking whim of hers, especially with the way she'd been staring earlier at my Rolex.

When we get to the cemetery I have to ask workmen for

directions to Pop's gravesite since this is the first time I've been there since the funeral. By this time I've calmed down; my mom, though, is still stewing in her resentment, an icy frigidness coming off her in waves, all over some fucking flowers. About what I should've expected. Anyway, I don't care.

I find Pop's grave. I wait by it while my mom plods along behind me. Pop's buried in a family plot, Tony and Jim are buried there also, although with Tony the casket's empty since the army was never able to locate his remains. There are two empty graves there waiting for my mom and me.

When my mom catches up, I hand her the roses to place on the graves. She puts six roses on Pop's, three each on my brothers'. All three gravestones are modest. With my pop's, just his name and the years marking his birth and death. Both Tony and Jim's have them being loving sons, and in Tony's case, that he died in service of his country. While we stand there, I see a wetness around my mom's eyes, then a few tears crawling down her cheek. It's a struggle but she keeps her mouth from crumbling.

We stand at the gravesite for around fifteen minutes, neither of us saying anything. My mom turns first to leave.

While we're walking to the car I spot a name on a gravestone that I recognize. It's a guy I hit for Lombard. The gravestone talks about what a wonderful person he was, a loving father and devoted husband. I remembered him as a cocaine-snorting asshole who fucked every whore he could get his dick into. He sold drugs for Lombard, and when DiGrassi found that this scumbag had been ripping Lombard off for five years I was brought into the picture. This loving father offered me his thirteen-year-old daughter to do whatever I wanted with as a way to try to save his ass. I didn't mind icing him one fucking bit.

I realize my mom's watching me. From the glimmer in her eyes, she knows that I had something to do with this fucker's death, probably even knows then what I do to make my money.

Christ, she's perceptive. Always has been able to look inside me, which pretty much explains why we don't like to be around each other.

chapter 20

present

I woke up with my head splitting. Squeezing my eyes hard against the sunlight drenching the room, I lay immobilized for a long minute before I sat up slowly, making sure to move at a glacier's pace to keep those tiny silver daggers from ripping into my brain any more than they were. Once I maneuvered myself into a sitting position, I cradled my head in my hands until I thought I could move. I realized then my cell phone was ringing but there wasn't a chance I'd be able to reach for it. Instead, each ring sent those daggers ripping deeper into my brain. When I could finally get off the bed, I stumbled to the bathroom and splashed cold water on to my face. I was still doing that when my cell phone rang again. Grabbing a towel to dry off my face, I went back to get the phone.

My eyes weren't functioning well enough for me to read the caller ID and I croaked into the phone instead, asking what the fuck the person wanted.

"Dad, is that you?"

It was my son, Michael. I sat on the edge of the bed and

carefully massaged my eyes with my thumb and forefinger. I apologized to him for the way I answered the call.

"This guy keeps calling and making vague, tough-guy threats," I explained. "I thought it was him calling again."

"Are you okay?" Michael asked. "You don't sound good."

"I'm okay. I just get these headaches. Today it's worse than usual."

"How long have you been getting them?"

"A long time. Years. It's nothing to worry about."

His voice flat, he said, "I'm not worried. I saw you on the news last night."

"I thought you don't watch TV?"

"Usually I don't. A co-worker called me to tell me about it." There was a pause, then, "If you want to meet me, I can do it today at twelve-thirty. Well?"

"Sure, I'd like that."

"I'll give you an address then, where we can meet."

"Okay, sure, let me get a pencil and paper."

Opening my eyes against the light was agony as a flood of tiny silver daggers emerged and went flying through my eyeballs and into my brain, but I ignored them as best I could and fumbled around the apartment until I found a pencil and some paper to write on, then had Michael give me the address of a coffee shop in Medfield. I knew nothing about Medfield other than that it was a good twenty miles away.

I asked, "Is that where you're living now?"

"No, but it's not too far from where I'm working. You should call the police about those phone calls you're getting."

"Yeah, I'll probably do that."

There was a click then as my son got off the line. I waited until my eyes could focus enough for me to dial, then I made several calls to find out how I could take the bus from Waltham to Medfield. It was going to require two bus transfers, which would leave me in Walpole, and from there I'd have to either walk four miles or take a cab, but I'd be able to get there by twelve-thirty. I made my way into the kitchen area where I poured several large glasses of lukewarm water down my throat, made a mental note that I needed to buy myself a coffee maker, then stumbled back to the bathroom. After stripping off my underwear I stood under the shower until my head started feeling more normal. At one point I tried lifting my right arm. My shoulder was sore as hell, but I was able to lift my arm higher than I could the other day, which was about all I could ask for.

When I got out of the shower I didn't have much time before I needed to catch the bus to meet my son. Despite how empty my stomach was feeling I didn't have time to make myself breakfast, so on the way to the bus stop I stopped off at a convenience store and bought a large coffee, a box of chocolate-glazed doughnuts and a newspaper.

I wished I had remembered my baseball cap and sunglasses, but I'd been in too big a rush and had left them back in my apartment. There weren't a lot of people on the sidewalk, but most of those that were turned my way as I went past them, and from the way their jaws dropped, there was no question that they recognized me. I was in too much of a hurry to care. As it was, I barely caught my bus. There was an empty seat in the back row that I took, and as was common with people who regularly take public transportation, most of the riders already sitting didn't bother looking up as I walked past them. The few that did didn't pay enough attention to recognize me.

Once I was seated I wolfed down two doughnuts and half the coffee. It made me feel a little better, my headache more its normal dull ache than the stabbing torturous pain it had been earlier. I reached into my pocket for my bottle of aspirin and realized I'd left that back in the apartment as well. Fuck it, I decided at this point it didn't matter. I'd be able to make it through the day okay without it.

As much as I was dreading it, I looked at the newspaper. Sure enough, I was back on the front page, and of course they had to prominently display a photo of me taken from the video that had been made. It was a long article which carried over to several pages. I tried reading it but the text blurred too much. I drank the rest of the coffee, sat back and closed my eyes. Ten minutes later I tried again. I had to hold the paper a few inches from my eyes, but this time I was able to focus enough on the print to read it.

The article dredged up all the stuff from the previous weeks, but grudgingly labeled what I did the other day "heroic", especially after finding out about the arrest records of the two Mueller brothers, who turned out to be fraternal twins. At nineteen they had robbed a liquor store and pistol-whipped the owner and two customers, and each ended up doing a four-year stretch for that. The police were now looking at them for a recent robbery in Watertown where the perps wore ski masks and an employee at the liquor store had been shot and beaten unconscious.

I went through the article carefully. There were quotes from Captain Edmund Gormer, all complimentary to me, and no hint that at any time I'd been a suspect. The paper had to counter all of that with past quotes from my victims' relatives. I guess it's easier going from hero to villain than the other way around. Anyway, I got some mild satisfaction from a picture that they included of the Mueller brothers as they were being booked for a host of offenses, both with the same fixed empty gazes in their eyes that you see on every hardened con.

When I was done with the article, I put the paper down and closed my eyes, and tried to remember what Michael looked like. For the life of me, all I could picture was the way he was when he was five years old and I took him to his first Red Sox game. Back then I spent whatever free time I could with him and Allison.

The cab driver recognized me. He was about my age; wispy gray hair framing a square-shaped skull, thick caterpillar eyebrows, rubbery features, near-impossible-to-understand Russian accent. I think he smelled even worse than I did when I first got out of prison. When I entered the cab, he explained away his bad body odor by telling me that he was in the middle of a second straight shift. "Thirteen hours so far in car," he announced proudly in his thick accent. Soon after we drove off, he started glancing at me through the rear-view mirror, his eyes befuddled under those massive eyebrows.

"You the person on TV," he said. "One who caught two hoodlums. Beat them up good too."

I didn't say anything.

He nodded to himself, sure of his recognition. "I saw you on TV, right before I start driving last night," he said. I caught the shift in his eyes as he remembered the rest of the story, about what I had done before and all the people I had murdered. He didn't say anything after that, and I could see the tremor in his hands as he gripped the wheel. Mercifully, it was a short cab ride. When I paid him the fare he avoided eye contact with me, and kept his lips pressed shut when I stiffed him on the tip.

From what I could tell of the little I saw of Medfield it appeared to be a quiet, quaint town. At one point it must've been mostly farmland, and still had a country feel to it. The coffee shop I was let out in front of was a modest, brightly yellow-painted Colonial that was probably until recently a family residence, and inside it looked more like an antique store than a coffee shop. Michael sat at a table facing the door, his features tense, his eyes fixed on me as I walked in. He had two cups of coffee in front of him, and he picked both of them up as he came to meet me. Before entering the shop I'd been debating whether to try for an embrace or to offer a handshake when we saw each other, but with both his hands full neither was possible. I followed him outside to an antique-looking cast-iron bench by the side of the building where we could talk without being overheard.

After we both sat on the bench he handed me one of the coffees, and I offered him a doughnut, which he accepted.

"Why'd you do that yesterday?" he asked. "Was it to impress me and Allie? Or were you just trying to get yourself killed?"

I shook my head. "I don't know, Michael. When I saw those two men standing outside the liquor store, I knew what they were going to do, and knew how it could turn out, and it just seemed like something I had to do. I wasn't trying to impress anyone or get myself hurt, it was just something that happened."

He sat quietly digesting what I told him, then said, "You wanted a chance to talk, so go ahead."

Even without the way he had been anxiously waiting for me inside the store, even without any clear memories of him except as a five-year-old child, I would've recognized him from Jenny. As soon as I saw Michael memories flooded back to me of how Jenny used to look. He had so much of my wife's soft features in his face. On Jenny, they were attractive and added to her femininity, on him they didn't look so good. They made him look weak, especially having Jenny's delicate mouth and slight chin. And with his ill-fitting suit and two days' stubble he looked shabby. I didn't mention any of that. Instead I told him it was good to see him.

"So it's good seeing me, what else do you want?" he demanded with some anger, his eyes hard glass as he looked at me.

"For Chrissakes, Michael. It's been over fourteen years. Give me a break here. I just want to know how you've been."

He took a long sip of his coffee before saying under his breath, "How do you think I'd be? How do you think anyone would be finding out at nineteen that their emotionally distant father was a cold-blooded psychopath and mass murderer?"

I sat back trying to make sense of this. It was hard to imagine that anyone would let their father's crimes against total strangers have such an effect on their own life, and it was even harder to imagine that someone with this much weakness and self-pity could have my blood in him. I felt an overwhelming sadness as I looked at Michael and knew that I was responsible for him being like this. He was a quiet kid, always serious-minded, but also good-natured. Physically he took after Jenny so much that I knew I needed to shelter him. That was why when he was four I moved the family to an upper-middle-class neighborhood, and that was why I sent him and Allison to private school. Because of that Michael didn't develop any toughness growing up and never had to learn how to fight. All of this weakness that I saw in him now was my fault.

"I wish your mom hadn't told you about what was in my confession," I said. "She should've just told you I was arrested for that extortion racket."

"And that would've been so much better, just thinking that you were a violent criminal? But for your information, Mom didn't tell us about any of that. FBI agents questioned all of us after you gave your statement. They were the ones who let us know about the people you murdered. I guess they thought it was part of their due diligence in verifying what you told them."

Jenny had never told me that. I couldn't help feeling some anger thinking about what the FBI did.

"I'm sorry that's the way you had to find out about me," I said.

"And what would've been a preferred way?" Michael's eyes had been fixed on me since we'd been sitting. A weariness dimmed the anger in them and he looked away from me, lowering his stare to the floor.

"To answer your question," he said, his voice showing the same weariness that had taken over his eyes, "I've been in and out of therapy for fourteen years, my marriage dissolved after three years, I have a kid that I'm not allowed to see, and I'm a recovering drug addict. It's only been in the last two years that I've gotten any sort of life together. So that's how I've been."

"I'm so sorry," I said, "I tried to give you a good home. And I made sure there would be enough money for college—"

"You don't get it," he said, his voice rising as he interrupted me, his eyes once again meeting mine. "How the fuck can you explain to me what you did?"

"It was a job—"

"Murdering people is a job? That's how you're going to explain it to me?"

I felt tongue-tied as I tried to come up with something to tell him. "These weren't nice people that I took out," I stammered out. My voice broke on me and I had to stop for a moment to take a sip of my coffee. I shifted uncomfortably in my seat, then looked back at Michael and saw how still he had become as he stared back at me. I looked away again, and after clearing my throat, continued.

"They were all in the life," I half mumbled, half said. "They knew the risks and dangers, just like I did. If I didn't take them out, Lombard would've hired someone else to do it. I was just doing a job, that's all."

"You're going to use the old Nazi excuse, that you were

just following orders? That would've made Grandma proud, wouldn't it!"

That was a low blow considering how my mom lost almost all of her family in concentration camps. I tried joking it off, though, telling him there wasn't a thing I could ever've done to have made my mom proud. Michael sat staring at me, unmoved.

"This was so long ago, Michael," I said. "I was a different person back then, and so much has happened since. But even still, I always cared about you, Allie, Paul and your mother. I never wanted to do anything to hurt any of you. Can't we move on from all that?"

"So your explanation is that you have no explanation," he said, more to himself than to me.

"That's not it," I said. "I tried the best I could for all of you. There's got to be a way we can put what I did in the past and talk about other stuff." I stopped for a moment, still tongue-tied, still feeling like I had a mouth full of marbles, then more to change the subject than anything else, asked him what he did for work.

Michael shook his head, said, "That's not something I want to tell you."

He didn't say this peevishly or with anger, just matter-of-factly, his eyes lost as he stared off into the distance. Awkwardly, I asked him about Allison and Paul, whether he kept in touch with them and if he could tell me how they were. Almost as if he were waking up from a dream, he looked at me and shook his head. "I'm not telling you about them either," he said.

"Is there anything about your life I can ask you?" I said.

"No, I don't think so."

He got up to leave, took several steps, then stopped, his lips twisting into an uneasy smile.

"Yeah, there is something I'd like to know," he said. "After Mom died, how'd you keep getting my phone numbers?"

"I used a service," I said.

He thought about that, nodded to himself. "Did you get more than just my phone numbers? Like maybe my addresses and pictures of me and my wife and kid?" he asked.

"No, all I could afford was your phone number. Allison's also."

"What about Paul's?"

"I tried, but the service I used couldn't find him."

He nodded again, a distant look on his face. "Good for Paul," he said. He turned his back on me and started to walk away.

"This isn't healthy for you, Michael," I called out. "We should talk this through."

He waved his hand angrily as if swatting at a swarm of gnats, and kept walking. I watched him until he was out of sight and knew I'd never see him again. I wondered briefly if there was any chance I'd ever see Allison or Paul, but accepted that that wasn't much more than wishful thinking, especially after the way Michael had acted. Of the three of them, he was always the peacemaker, the one who would try to smooth out hard feelings and get people talking again. If he couldn't forgive me there wasn't much chance the other two ever would.

I sat for a long moment feeling a weakness in my legs and an emptiness filling up my chest. For a moment it was as if I were drowning in it. Then I decided to stop feeling sorry for myself. I don't know what else I could've been expecting from him, not with the way he ignored my calls when I was in prison and left those early letters of mine unanswered – the ones I wrote when Jenny was still alive to forward them to him – and not with the way Jenny would change the subject whenever I'd bring up Michael or the other two kids.

I got myself to my feet and decided to walk the four miles to the bus stop. It wasn't as if I had any place to be, and I figured the walk could help clear my head and maybe loosen some of the stiffness I was feeling in my shoulder. I thought about Michael's comment about me being "emotionally distant". I certainly wasn't when my kids were young. Maybe later there was some truth to that, especially when I started becoming paranoid that they'd be able to smell the stench of death on me. Or maybe it happened later after they became teenagers – maybe that was when I felt like I couldn't relate to them any longer. I don't know.

I glanced upwards for a brief moment towards the sun before looking away. Christ, I wished I had worn my baseball cap and sunglasses, especially with the way the sunlight made my skull feel like a vise was being tightened around it. I thought about seeing if anyone inside the coffee shop could spare some aspirin, but decided against doing that, thinking that someone there might've overheard part of my conservation with Michael and not feeling up to facing any of those people right then. Instead, I took off on foot to retrace the path that the cab driver had taken.

I waited over an hour for the first bus, then close to another hour for the second one. The day so far had worn me down, and at some point while riding back to Waltham I dozed off. The next thing I was aware of was a presence taking the seat next to me. A familiar voice then asked me for my autograph. I opened my eyes a crack and saw Sophie Duval, a brightness in her eyes and her lips curved into a thin smile while she studied me. Once I realized who she was I turned away quickly to wipe off some drool that I felt running down the side of my mouth, then I told her that I charged more than she could afford.

"I wouldn't doubt it," she said. "Especially after your heroics from yesterday. That was quite a video they showed on TV."

"I haven't had a chance to see it yet," I lied.

"You should. It's impressive. Vintage Chuck Norris-type stuff. And best of all, you left the talking heads on TV baffled. They don't know what to make of you any more."

Any other beautiful young woman sitting next to me would've sat tensed and compact in their seat, making sure there would be no bodily contact with me. Sophie, on the other hand, sat relaxed with her arm and leg lightly touching mine. As I mentioned before, part of her con required her to hint at a vague promise of sex, or at least intimacy.

"It's a pleasant surprise seeing you on this bus," I said.

"An even bigger one for me," she said. "I thought I was seeing things when I walked onboard and saw you back here snoozing away. I would've thought reporters would be all over you for interviews."

"They probably would be if they knew where to find me." I glanced out the window trying to get some sense of bearing but was unable to recognize where we were. It wasn't rural like Medfield, but we weren't in Waltham either, at least not so I could tell. "What are you doing out here?" I asked.

"A job prospect," she said.

"Did it go well?"

"We'll see." She leaned in close to me and rested her hand lightly on mine. The feel of her skin was electric. With her brow furrowed and her voice low, she whispered to me, "Leonard, you should be more careful about falling asleep in public. I'm sure that car was following you a few days ago. And I'm sure you have more than your share of enemies."

I nodded, acknowledging her concern. She relaxed back in her seat, still keeping her arm and leg touching mine. Even though there was fabric separating our skin, the touch of her made me lightheaded. We sat making small talk, mostly her joking about how I should get a set of action figures marketed for myself; that with enough publicity I could be the next Rambo. After we entered Waltham, I caught a glimpse of a calculating shine in her eyes, and I waited for what I knew was coming. We were maybe two blocks from our stop when she mentioned about how when we first met I had asked her if she was a writer.

I nodded slowly.

She said, "I don't have any training as one, but your story is amazing, especially after what you did yesterday. Leonard, with the two of us working together I'm sure we could still write a kickass book, one that we could get paid a lot of money for. I mean, how hard could it be? And who knows, maybe we'd even be able to get a movie deal for it. So what do you say?"

"I'll have to think about it," I said, my voice catching on me.

"Please do." She placed her hand again on top of mine. "I've been going though a rough patch, to put it lightly, and this could really bail me out. And it would be so much fun. Think of it, Leonard, the two of us getting to work hard through all those nights together."

I should've turned her down. But the thing was, even though she was just playing me, and had only been playing me ever since we met, I knew something that she didn't. That there was a genuine connection between us. I didn't know exactly what it was, but I could feel it just as much as I could feel the electricity of her touch. No matter how good a con artist she was, and she was damn good, she couldn't have felt as comfortable with me as she did without that connection existing, and I knew that part of it wasn't an act. I didn't say anything. I couldn't.

"Can we meet tomorrow and talk about it?" she asked,

a faint pleading in her voice. "Maybe you can give it some thought tonight?"

"Sure," I said.

A hint of a sly smile showed on her face then. We agreed on where and when to meet, and after the bus rolled into our stop we walked together with her arm hooked through mine until it was time for us to go our separate ways. I stood still and watched as she walked down a side street, a lump forming in my throat. I should've turned her down since I knew there was no way I was ever going to let a book be written about me, at least with my help. I couldn't do it, though. Just as she was playing me I was going to have to play her as long as I could. If I could buy another week or two of her needing to meet with me, maybe by then she'd understand the connection between us too.

I found myself already looking forward to when I'd see her the next day.

I was near dead on my feet by the time six o'clock came around, and decided to treat myself to a steak dinner. The restaurant I went to wasn't fancy or anything, but it was several cuts above the places I had been eating. My waiter clearly recognized me from how nervous he acted. He didn't say anything to me, though, not even to take my order, just stood sweating and looking like he was about to keel over. Before too long other diners were shooting furtive glances my way, and I heard their hushed whispers, but none of them said anything directly to me either. I didn't care. I ignored them all, and after a sirloin steak, baked potato, piece of apple pie with vanilla ice cream, and half a dozen cups of black coffee, I felt mostly rejuvenated and up to working my job.

That night the kid working security avoided eye contact when I checked out the office keys, his mouth forming a sullen, hurt look. I decided I preferred it this way than to listening to any of his smartass cracks. My shoulder was still sore and I couldn't lift it any higher than I could that morning, but it didn't slow me down and I was able to keep my usual pace. The talk shows were still talking about what I did the other day, and the calls were still all over the place about my motive, with some callers suggesting I had some nefarious reason for avoiding the reporters who've been wanting to interview me about the incident. I listened to them for the first hour, then switched over to music.

Later, as I was vacuuming the offices I thought I heard voices again drifting in from the lobby, but by the time I turned the vacuum off they were gone. This time I didn't bother checking it out.

Chapter 21

1985

I can still smell that dense, musky smell coming from my skin.

I've been sitting in the steam room at the Y off and on for over two hours now and I can't seem to sweat it out of me. Deep down I know the smell doesn't really exist, that it's some sort of obsessive compulsive thing going on, but it doesn't help me much. I took the target out hours ago. It was a clean hit, too. No witnesses, no surprises, not even a drop of blood on me.

I play the hit over in my mind. The guy I took out is a piece of shit, and nobody's going to be missing him much. I have no remorse over what I did. This isn't anything like that. No guilt is eating away at me. It's just that when I smell that odor, even if I know it's only in my mind, I don't want my kids anywhere near me. I can't help feeling that if I have any physical contact with them, I'll get that stench all over them too, and I don't want to stain them that way. Even if I know it's all just in my head.

And that's the rub. Because today is Paul's sixth birthday. Jenny's throwing a party for him, something she's been planning for a while now, and I promised her I'd be there. And fuck, I want to be there. But then I had to get that call last night. Sal Lombard needed the hit done this morning. I couldn't argue with him. He's not the type of man you can argue with. Besides, I wouldn't have had any good reason for postponing it. The hit went down easy and all it should mean is once less piece of scum in the world.

I leave the steam room to go back to the showers where I scrub myself under hot water for a good fifteen minutes. This is the third time I've done this. After I turn off the water I inhale deeply. The stench is faint, but it's still there. Me, personally, I couldn't care less about it, but I just don't want it on my kids. As it is I know they sense something about me, at least Michael and Allison do. Michael's always been a quiet and moody kid, and the last year it's like he skulks around when he's near me, never saying more than two words to me, at least not voluntarily. It breaks my heart having him like that.

Something's up with Allison too. She always used to be Daddy's little girl, always jumping into my lap when I'm trying to read the racing forms or watching TV. She doesn't do that any more. Hasn't for months now. Recently I've been catching this odd look on her, like she's not quite sure what to make of me.

Jenny knows something's not right with me and these two kids. She doesn't say anything to me about it, but I can see the questioning looks she gives me when those two start moping around in my presence, like I'm abusing them or something. Nothing could be further from the truth. I've never once laid a hand on either of them. Never raised my voice either. So I ignore those looks Jenny gives me. What am I going to tell her? How am I going to explain that those two have a bad feeling about me? Christ, it doesn't make any sense. Even the family cat still crawls into my arms as if I'm a decent person.

Those two kids somehow see something that the cat doesn't, or at least they think they do.

Paul's different than Michael and Allison. Whatever it is that the other two kids think they know about me, he's oblivious to it. Maybe it's because he takes after me while the other two have so much of Jenny in them. With Allison it's a good thing, you can see that she's going to grow up to be a beautiful woman. Even with Michael I guess it's probably good too; maybe he'll escape having to be the same ugly fuck I am.

Paul, though, he's already a miniature version of me. Short and thin and wiry, and with this ferociousness about him. He's half the size of Michael, and only six years old to Michael's eleven, but I'd still bet money on Paul having a first-round knockout if the two of them ever got into a fight. But there's not much chance of that ever happening – whenever Paul tries pushing Michael into a fight, Michael backs down, and as much as he tries to pretend otherwise, it's out of fear, not restraint.

I head back to the steam room to try to sweat out the last faint remnants of that stench, and I see from a clock on the wall that the party has already been underway for over an hour. I doubt it will still be going on by the time I head home. Jenny's going to be disappointed, but she won't say anything to me about it. She stopped voicing her disappointment years ago, besides, she knows whatever excuse I give her will be a lie. Anyway, deep down inside the last thing she wants is any hint of the truth. Paul, on the other hand, won't let it faze him one way or the other. With Michael and Allison this will be one more grudge for them to hold against me.

I take a seat in the steam room and close my eyes, my head lowered, a towel hanging loosely around my neck. I don't have much left to sweat out, but what else am I going to do?

If only I hadn't gotten that call last night…

chapter 22

present

At nine o'clock the next morning someone knocked on my door. When I didn't answer it, the person knocked harder and shouted through the door, announcing himself as Eric Slaine, a reporter for one of the local Boston papers. I put away the book I had been reading and pushed myself out of the recliner. If Lombard's boys had figured out where I was living, they wouldn't bother with a trick like pretending they were a reporter to get me to open the door – they would just kick it down.

I opened the door enough to look out. Standing in the hallway was a kid in his thirties, about my size, dressed casually in jeans and a turtleneck sweater. As thin and short as he was, he was good-looking with thick brown hair and the type of pretty-boy looks a lot of girls go for. He also looked damned pleased with himself as he stood there smirking at me.

He introduced himself again and held out a hand for me. When I didn't take it, it didn't deter him in the slightest. All it did was make his expression all the more smug.

"Leonard March," he said, whistling softly to himself. "I've been looking nonstop for you for over a day now. What will it take to let me interview you about what happened outside Donnegan's Liquors?"

He was lying to me. It couldn't have been true about him looking nonstop for me, not with how refreshed he looked. He had clearly had a good night's sleep. He'd also taken the time in the morning to shave and shower, and not a hair was out of place. You could tell he wasn't someone who was ever going to skimp on his personal appearance. Instinctively, I didn't like him.

"How'd you find me?" I asked.

"A professional secret," Slaine said.

"If you were able to find me, others will too, and these will be people who are going to want something other than an interview. So why don't you quit acting cute and tell me if someone's selling my address."

I didn't need him to tell me that. I already knew somebody was. While it was no mystery that I was living in Waltham, nobody should've known my address, at least outside of my prison caseworker, Theo Ogden, and whoever had access to the apartment building's administrative files. The story I was given about pest maintenance being in my apartment was bullshit. My place had been searched by professionals the other day, and I wanted to know whether Theo or someone else was giving out my address.

Slaine considered what I asked him. "I'll trade you," he said. "You give me an interview and I'll tell you how I found you."

Looking at him I could feel the heat rising off the back of my neck, especially with how much more smug his smile had gotten.

"If you're going to be knocking on doors expecting favors from people the least you can do is answer a civil question," I said. "And show some consideration. What the fuck are you doing knocking on doors at nine in the morning, especially given that people might've been working late the night before?"

"You have a job, huh?" he asked pleasantly. "And you're working nights, too. Mind my asking where?"

I started to close the door on him, but he moved a foot into the doorway to block me, then squeezed his shoulder through the opening. I didn't fight him as he muscled the door open and pushed his way forward, only stopping when his face was inches from mine.

"I showed you more consideration than you showed the people you murdered," he said, his voice tight, his breath sour as if he'd been eating chopped herring. He was still smirking at me, but there was no humor in his eyes any more and his skin color had dropped a shade. "About waking you up – I didn't think there was much chance of that, at least not after talking to prison officials about you and finding out about your sleep habits. So Leonard, let's quit the bullshit. What's your cost for an interview?"

"Two things," I said. "First, tell me how you found me."

"Fair enough," he agreed. "I went to every low-rent apartment building starting near Donnegan's Liquors, and showed your picture around until I found you at this dump. What else?"

"Ten thousand dollars. In cash and off the books."

He didn't bat an eye at that price. "I'll have to talk to my supervisor," he said. "But for that amount of money we're going to want a lot more than what went down at that liquor store. We're going to want to know about your life as a hit man for the mob and your time in prison."

"Okay."

He stepped away from the doorway and rolled his shoulders

in order to adjust his turtleneck sweater. "Why don't you give me your phone number so I can call when I get an answer about your price?" he asked.

I shook my head. "Leave me a card and I'll call you next week."

He looked like he wanted to argue with me about that, but he reluctantly fished a card out of his wallet and handed it to me. "For ten grand it's going to have to be an exclusive interview," he warned me. "You can't be talking to anybody else."

I watched him walk away before I closed the door shut. When I gave him that ten grand figure I never expected him to be able to meet it, I just threw out that number to get him away from me. I stared at his card for a long minute trying to decide what to do with it. I wanted to rip it up – I sure as fuck didn't want to do an interview – but I started thinking about what I could do with ten grand if I could get it paid to me under the table, and Sophie figured in the equation. If it wasn't for her the money wouldn't have even been a thought. In the end, I stored the card away instead of tossing it like I had first intended.

There was only one person who knew the truth about any of the things I'd done, and that was me. If they were able to come up with ten grand and I decided to go along with an interview, whatever I gave them would be better put to use as fertilizer.

I had an hour before I was going to be meeting Sophie. I stripped off the ratty clothes I'd put on when I first woke up, took a long shower, shaved, then splashed on some new aftershave I'd bought the evening before. After that, I put on a new pair of slacks, shirt and sweater that I had dropped two bills for at a local department store after I had left Sophie the other day.

I stepped outside and pulled the collar of my leather jacket tight against my neck. The weather had turned colder with the sun nowhere in sight and the skies darkened by thick purplish-grayish clouds. Sophie and I were going to meet in a park near Moody Street. I hadn't been there before but I followed her directions, walking briskly with my head lowered and my hands buried deep in my jacket pockets.

The park was empty when I arrived there. There wasn't much to it: a few benches, a swing set, a small area of dead grass. As I made my way to one of the benches I saw Sophie off in the distance. I smiled at that. As good as she'd been so far with the con she still had things to learn. The smart play would've been to keep me waiting at least a half-hour to get me more invested. Anyway, I waved to her and she waved back.

Her hair was as much a hornet's nest as every other time I'd seen her, and she looked even colder than I felt in her threadbare cloth coat and jeans that weren't in much better shape. I couldn't help feeling a jitteriness in my stomach as I watched her hustling towards me carrying a paper bag under one of her arms. When she joined me on the bench she handed me the bag while she rubbed her hands together and blew into them. Inside the bag were two large coffees and cream cheese bagels wrapped up in paper. I handed Sophie one of the coffees, then unwrapped a bagel and cream cheese to hand her as well. We sat quietly eating our sandwiches and drinking our coffee, but it was a comfortable quiet. When we were done Sophie commented that it was nice having breakfast with someone for a change, then glanced up at the sky and remarked how it might start raining soon.

"That would put a dampener on things," I said.

She got a laugh out of that. "Yes, it certainly would," she agreed.

"How come a beautiful girl like you doesn't have someone to share breakfast with?" I asked.

She smiled at that. It was a sad, almost tragic smile, and it made me think again about my original thought of her having done time in prison, and I couldn't help feeling that that was probably what had happened, and maybe it was only recently that she had gotten out. It would explain a lot, especially the connection I knew we had.

"Leonard," she said softly, but with a heavy breath, "that would be a long and complicated story, one I could write a book on. And I have to thank you for the 'beautiful' compliment, although I certainly don't deserve it. Also for thinking that I could be young enough to be thought of as a 'girl'. How old do you think I am?"

"Twenty-five," I lied.

"You're ten years off, my friend."

"You're only fifteen?" I said, raising an eyebrow in mock surprise. "Chrissakes, I could get myself thrown back into prison for corrupting a minor."

The word "prison" put a dampener on her mood, and for a few seconds a darkness clouded her face to a color that came close to matching the skies. Then just as quickly it was gone. I couldn't help feeling something bad had happened to her when she was young, and I wanted to ask her about it but I didn't want to hear what I knew she would tell me: that she had been abused at one time in her life and ended up serving time for manslaughter or maybe even second-degree murder. Instead I sat there tongue-tied, feeling an awkward silence between us.

She reached over and took hold of my hand and squeezed it, the way a friend would, and just like that, knocked away any of the awkwardness that we had started to feel.

"You're a charmer, Leonard," she said. "But as you well know, I'm thirty-five, and it hasn't been the easiest thirty-five years so far. Not exactly the fairy-tale princess life I'd dreamed about when I was a very young child."

"The next thirty-five then," I said.

She nodded solemnly at that. "The next thirty-five it will be," she agreed.

"If you want to tell me anything, feel free," I said. I forced a rigid smile. "I'm not exactly someone who could hold you or anyone else in judgment."

"There's not much to tell," she said. "Bad stuff happened to me as a child, I ended up in foster homes, then much worse stuff happened. Now I'm in Waltham trying to figure out what to do with my life, and I meet you." She paused for a moment, then asked, "Leonard what were your parents like? Were they the reason you ended up working for the mob?"

From her tone and the hopefulness in her eyes, she was really searching for why her own life had taken the course that it did, because if I had made my wrong turn due to environmental factors maybe she had also. Maybe there wasn't something seriously broken in either of us. It would've been easy to lie to her; instead, though, I shook my head.

"My parents? No. Hardly. My pop was what you'd call a salt o'the earth type. As honest and decent as the day is long. A good man who never had a harsh word for anyone, and sweated blood every day as he worked his way to an early grave."

"Your mom, then?"

"My mom and I never got along," I admitted. "She had a hard life herself, lots of tragedies and losses, but she had nothing to do with me working for the mob either. They gave me a good home. Whatever happened was my doing."

The skies opened up then, the rain coming down hard and suddenly as if a faucet had been turned on full. I took my jacket off so Sophie could use it to shield herself. We ran the two blocks back to Moody Street, stopping only when we were under an awning. Even with my jacket sheltering her Sophie had still gotten soaked and was looking a bit like a drowned rat. I was so winded I had a hard time breathing, and thought at first that I might be having a heart attack, but the moment passed and my breathing became less ragged.

Sophie handed me back my jacket. With a heartbreaking smile, she said, "What a mess we are, huh? Leonard, dear, I'm sorry you got so wet, but it was very chivalrous of you. I thank you."

She looked so miserable standing there with her hair hanging down in wet tangled clumps and her threadbare jacket and jeans soaked through. She had also started to shiver. I ignored her protests and draped my leather jacket around her thin shoulders, then told her there was a store a block over where I was going to buy her a new jacket.

"I can't let you do that," she said.

"I wouldn't worry about it. Think of it as a gift from the Waltham Police."

That got her curious, and I explained how the police had first tried to tie me up with an assault charge after I had broken up the attempted liquor store robbery, and later how I squeezed a hundred and fifty dollars out of them. Even with the way she was shivering I could tell that she enjoyed the story.

"I can't think of a better way of spending that money," I told her.

She didn't put up a fight over it, and we made our way through the rain to the next block by darting in and out of doorways and under awnings for protection. When we got to the department store, I first bought a beach towel, which we used to dry ourselves off, then I helped Sophie pick out a ski jacket. It was bulky on her and hid her curves, which was a shame, but it was waterproof, had a hood, and offered much better protection from the cold than what she'd been wearing.

When she put it on she gave me one of the brightest smiles I'd ever seen. Yeah, it was going to cost me a hundred and seventy dollars and my funds were dwindling, but it was worth the price. And besides, if I got ten grand for that interview, money wasn't going to be much of an issue, at least not for a while.

The rain was still coming down in sheets and Sophie insisted that I also buy an umbrella for myself. When I took the jacket and umbrella to the cash register, the cashier gave us a puzzled look as he tried to figure out whether we were father and daughter, and if not, what the possible attraction might've been. I couldn't blame him. Based purely on our appearances we were as mismatched a couple as you could've found. After he handed me my change and we had him cut the tags off the jacket, we left him still trying to solve the mystery.

Once we were back outside and under the store's awning, Sophie put her new jacket on, including the hood, and zipped up, and we both stood quietly for a long moment watching the rain beating down even harder than before. Sophie spoke first, asking how she looked in her jacket.

"Like a million bucks," I told her.

She rolled her eyes at that. "Yeah, right." Her expression turned pensive, and she added, "Leonard, we never did talk about the two of us writing a book together."

I hesitated. I had planned to lie and keep my own little con going as long as Sophie was keeping hers, but I couldn't do it any more; besides, hers was no longer as much of a con as she probably thought it was.

I looked away from her. "I don't think us writing a book is possible," I said, my voice barely audible over the rain. "Monday I'm going to court for wrongful death suits that have been filed against me. Any money that we'd get on a book deal would end up getting attacked by the relatives behind these lawsuits. We wouldn't make any money off of it."

I couldn't look at her, nor could I move. My jaw clamped shut, and as I stood there, I felt a hollowness expanding throughout my chest, making me feel as if I could be crumpled as easily as a piece of tinfoil. I dreaded what I was about to lose. Seeing Sophie, even if it was only a game on her part, and even if it was only for a few spare minutes every couple of days, was one of the few things that allowed me to feel human.

I waited for her to leave me, but instead her hand found mine. The warmth and feel of it were dizzying.

"Leonard, I have to go away this weekend," she said. "Let's talk again on Monday after your court hearing. Maybe we'll figure something out, but even if we don't, at least it will give us a chance to see each other."

I nodded. I still couldn't look at her. I wanted to believe there was a genuineness in what she was saying, and that she wasn't just trying to keep the con going as long as there was still a glimmer of hope in pulling it off. From her voice it sounded like there was a chance that it was that way, but I didn't want to risk looking into her eyes and having my fantasy squashed.

We agreed on where and when to meet on Monday, then her lips touched lightly against my cheek as she kissed me.

"That was so sweet of you buying me this jacket," she said.

My head turned and I caught the look in her eyes. It wasn't just a con any more. Not entirely, anyway. She gave my hand one last squeeze so that her fingernails left small indentations in my skin, then, smiling weakly at me, she walked off into the rain. I stood silently and watched her as she hurried down the sidewalk and disappeared from sight. Minutes after she was gone I still stood silently as I thought things over. What I should've done next was head back to my apartment so I could take a shower and dry off properly. Instead, though, I trudged off to the public library.

It rained constantly that weekend. Saturday morning I felt like a caged animal as I stayed inside my apartment. I was too anxious to sit still, and pretty quickly gave up trying to read the book that I had picked up. My mind kept racing, both thinking about Sophie and what the zoo atmosphere was going be like when I went to the Chelsea District Courthouse on Monday. I also kept thinking about who would be there waiting for me.

I ate an early lunch, frying a sausage and cutting it up so I could add it to a can of minestrone soup, but in the state of mind I was in I could barely taste any of it. By one o'clock I found myself pacing the apartment, too agitated to do much else. I grabbed my jacket and umbrella then and ventured out to a local movie theatre that was a half-mile from my apartment. It was nasty walking with the rain coming down almost horizontally and the umbrella doing little to protect my pants legs and shoes, but I was glad to be out of my apartment, and even though my mind was drifting too much to follow the movie I ended up seeing, I felt better sitting in that dark room with noises and random images to distract me. It didn't matter that my head was hurting worse than usual and my pants and shoes were soaked – I felt more relaxed sitting there. Maybe it took me back to my childhood, I don't know. But I ended up sitting through two showings of the movie, and I couldn't tell you a thing about it.

After leaving the movie house, I stopped off at a bar for an early dinner and several beers. I could've had several more easily enough, but I had my job to go to later that night.

Later, when I showed up at the office building, there was a different man working security. He was just as tight-lipped as the kid who was usually there, and like the kid, didn't say a word to me as I checked out the keys. He wasn't any kid, though. He was at least my age, probably older, white hair framing a face that was as wrinkled as any turtle's.

Work went by fast. I had left my radio back in the apartment, not wanting to risk the rain damaging it. That night, though, I didn't mind the silence. It helped having all those menial tasks to focus my thoughts on, and I ended up finishing an hour early. I spent the extra hour sitting in a third-floor office and watching the rain come down. At two o'clock, when I checked the office keys back in, the old man filling in at security avoided eye contact with me, and I left the building without the two of us exchanging a single word.

The streets were desolate as I made my way back to my apartment. The only sign of life were some rats in an alleyway that had converged by an open garbage bin. I stopped to watch them for a while, then continued on.

That night I had an erotic dream about Sophie. The two of us were alone in an unfamiliar room. Sophie stood shivering in front of me, an uneasiness in her eyes, although she didn't say anything as I undressed her. My mouth became dry as I studied her thin but still near-perfect naked body; her slender hips, the slight bulge to her stomach, the small patch of pubic hair, her breasts – no bigger than a handful, but the sight of them making my head pound. While I looked her over, her olive complexion brightened to a crimson. I ran my thumb over her perfect pink nipples and felt them as they hardened.

I could see the pleading in her eyes as I lifted her and carried her to a bed, but she didn't say anything and any objections she might've had stayed buried in her throat. I positioned her so she was on her knees. Her skin was hot, nearly burning, and the feel of her small hips made me breathless. I penetrated her from behind and I pushed myself over and over again into her, the only sound coming from her being soft gasps, maybe sobs, I wasn't sure which.

I woke up having stained my underwear. My erection grew soft, and I lay frozen, desperately trying to hold on to the way it felt in my dream being with Sophie and the way she had looked naked, but it was gone.

It was dark in my room. I stared bleary-eyed at my alarm clock until I could see that it was only four in the morning. I pushed myself out of bed, stripped off my underwear and washed it in the bathroom sink. After hanging it up to dry, I took a shower, then, after dressing, sat in my recliner and tried to read one of my books. My mind kept drifting too much to pay any attention to what I was trying to read, but I needed to do something to kill time until the sun came out.

chapter 23

1991

Fred Marzone's in the motel room next to me screwing the shit out of a hooker. I can hear them through the cheaply plastered wall, which is probably no thicker than a piece of cardboard. I know she's a hooker. I was watching Marzone's room from across the street when she arrived. Just a kid, really. Not much flesh on her, not enough anyway, her arms and legs looking like broomsticks with her dressed up in hot pants, a tube top, and cheap gold stiletto heels. Way too much makeup on her as well. It made me think of my daughter when she used to play dress-up.

It was lousy timing her showing up when she did. Marzone must know there's a hit on him; it's the only thing that explains why it's been such a pain in the ass tracking him down, and why he's holed up now at a fleabag roadside motel in Lynn. I'd only just found Marzone and was preparing myself to kick down his motel room door and put a few bullets in his head when I saw the hooker coming out of nowhere. I slipped back into the shadows then and watched as she walked hesitantly to his door and knocked on it, and then Marzone letting her in. After that I checked out the neighboring room, found that it was empty, and was able to easily pick the lock. Now I'm settled in and listening to her moaning while Marzone's grunting away like a rutting pig.

Lombard would probably be putting a hit on me if he knew I was sitting here waiting for them to finish up and for that hooker to leave instead of just busting in and icing the both of them. I can imagine what Lombard would be yelling at me if he knew what I was doing now. *Why the fuck you sittin' on your ass? For Chrissakes, who the fuck's going to give a shit about some crack addict whore? Do your goddamned job!*

It's almost like I can hear him growling in my ear. But the thought of taking out this skinny hooker with way too much makeup on makes me sick to my stomach, especially given that the kid's last few minutes are going to be taking Marzone's five inches up her ass. No one should have to die with that being their last few moments on earth. What's the harm in showing a little patience? So Marzone's brains will be blown out later tonight instead of right now, what's the harm in that?

They've been going at it over an hour. My stomach's knotting up more each minute as I sit there. I can't help worrying that the room I'm camped out in will be rented and I'll be forced to take out more victims than just Marzone. The smart play is to go in there now and take care of the situation, but I sit paralyzed thinking of how young the girl is and the sad, almost despair-ridden look I saw on her while she waited outside Marzone's door.

It hits me that I'm not hearing bedsprings squeaking any more, and that I haven't for a while now. There's still grunting and moaning and occasional voices whispering through the wall, but none of the squealing that the bed was making earlier. My blood runs cold as I strain to hear more of the voices coming from the other room and realize that's not Marzone in there – at least it's not the same voice I heard earlier.

A sweat dampens the back of my neck as I run out of the room. I check to make sure no one's watching, then while holding a .40 caliber subcompact in one hand, use my burglar's pick to unlock Marzone's door. The room's empty. The noises I'd been hearing are coming from the TV set. The sonofabitch had ordered up a porn movie and left it running while he took off.

I give the room a quick search. There was nothing personal left behind. Marzone's not coming back. That paranoid fuck must've left that porn movie running as a precaution. He couldn't have known anyone was next door listening in, because if it was anyone with half a brain they wouldn't have given a shit about the teenage hooker he was pounding away on.

I use the one clean towel in the rat-trap of a bathroom to wipe the sweat off the back of my neck and forehead, and try to think of what I'm going to tell Lombard. I know he paid good money for the tip off of where Marzone was, and I know he's not going to be happy when he finds out Marzone's still alive.

I curse myself out as I leave the room, and just hope Lombard will buy the load of bullshit I'll be giving him later.

chapter 24

present

Sunday was just one of those days to get through like all those days during my fourteen-year prison stretch. It was still raining hard, and I was sick of the wet and cold, but was feeling too antsy to stay caged inside my studio apartment. By noon I had to get out, and I made my way to Moody Street and found a cheap bar to camp out in. From one o'clock to ten in the evening football was on the TV, and I nursed a half dozen beers, had a greasy cheeseburger and fries, and stared vacantly at the TV. It wasn't quite the same watching football without having any action on the games, but at least it killed the day. At times I noticed people staring at me, but I didn't care whether they recognized me. They gave me a wide berth, and that was all I cared about.

Later, miraculously, I slept through the night, and woke up only when the alarm went off at six o'clock Monday morning. I lay disoriented before remembering where I was and what I had to do later that morning. Reaching over, I turned off the buzzer and forced myself out of bed. My court appearance was scheduled for ten o'clock. The previous week I had worked out the connecting buses I needed to take to get to the courthouse in Chelsea, and it required me to leave my apartment by seven-thirty.

I made myself a breakfast of bacon and scrambled eggs, along with toast, then took a shower, shaved, and changed into the cleanest clothes I had. A suit would've been desirable, but I didn't have one.

Saturday morning I had gotten another call from *unavailable*, and instead of answering it I had turned off my cell phone. I turned my phone back on and saw that I had seven messages waiting for me. I didn't bother checking them or the call log to see who they were from. Within minutes of turning the phone back on, it rang with the caller ID indicating again *unavailable*. This time I answered it, asking whoever it was what the fuck they wanted.

The same voice from the earlier calls chuckled lightly, said, "Answering your phone again, huh, March?"

"Why don't you just tell me what you want?"

"Not too much," he said. "Only to let you know that I'll be seeing you in court today. And afterwards too."

"You're such a tough guy," I said, "how about showing some balls and giving me your name?"

Whoever it was must've found some humor in my request. He broke into a wheezing laugh before telling me he'd be seeing me soon enough and I'd know his name then, and hung up.

I thought about turning off my phone again, but decided if he wanted to call me some more, let him. I found the court documents that were sent to me while I was in prison, gave them a cursory look, then took all of the papers I had with me as I headed off to catch the first bus I needed to take to get to Chelsea.

The bus let me off three blocks from the courthouse. The rain had stopped sometime Sunday night, and it was a crisp late October day. I had forty minutes before my scheduled court appearance, and the last thing I wanted to do was sit in a hall surrounded by an angry mob of my victims' relatives, so instead I found a small diner a block in the opposite direction of the courthouse and took a seat at the counter. There were several blue-collar types already sitting at the counter, all big heavy men who showed the kind of work they did by their dirt-stained fingernails. One by one they looked over at me, and as they did, I could see a faint glint of recognition in their eyes. That was it, though. They didn't show anything by their poker-faced expressions, nor did they say anything. They drank their coffee, while a couple of them also ignored the state-wide smoking ban as they let cigs burn between their fingers. One of them got up and casually headed towards the door, his pace quickening only once he got near it.

Through the storefront window I saw him take out a cell phone, then watched as he walked out of view. Whoever he was going to be calling it didn't much matter – I'd be heading back to court before they'd show up.

I nodded to the guy working the counter who from his demeanor probably also owned the place. He was a middle-aged man, barrel-chested, with a thick neck and a red face, and had on a stained tee shirt and an even more badly stained apron over a pair of khakis. A short buzz cut flattened out the top of his head. He stood to the side glowering at me, several blue-green tattoos expanding as he ominously flexed his arm muscles. He clearly didn't want to wait on me, but I asked him for some coffee anyway.

"We don't serve rats here," he said, a deep frown creasing his face, and his mouth puckered up to show his disgust.

I couldn't get over that. *We don't serve rats here.* It didn't matter that I had murdered all the people that I did, what he cared about was that I had ratted on Lombard. It just seemed so out of proportion, and I could feel my blood heating up and my steely old self coming to the fore, and I told him he'd better start learning how to. He wavered, not quite so sure of himself after that, and grudgingly poured me a cup of coffee. He didn't even spit in it as he pushed it towards me. The other customers sitting at the counter had picked up on my tone, and I could sense their growing nervousness. I looked over my shoulder at them and could see the tightness around each of their mouths as they struggled to maintain their nonchalant act. If I yelled *boo* at least one of them probably would've passed out on the spot. I looked away from them.

I sat quietly for the next ten minutes and drank my coffee. The place had become a tomb. All conversation had died. The man working the counter avoided looking in my direction, almost as if he was scared he'd turn to stone if he caught a glimpse of me, while the other blue-collar types at the counter were afraid to make any movement outside of a few anxious glances. All because I had let my old self out for a brief moment. When I finished my coffee I dropped a couple of dollars on the counter and left.

It was a few minutes before ten by the time I had arrived at the courthouse. Standing outside were two wiseguys. They both had the same hardened look about them, both dressed casually in jeans and sneakers; one wearing a leather bomber jacket, the other a New England Patriots windbreaker. They had on dark shades so I couldn't see their eyes, but there was no hiding that they were in the game, and my gut told me they worked for Lombard. I knew they were watching me as I entered the courthouse but they kept their distance. They could have just as well been carved out of granite by the way they stood unmoving and the cold deadness in their faces.

I was left alone as I walked through the courthouse, and it

wasn't until I reached the courtroom where my hearing was scheduled that I encountered an angry mob waiting for me. There were maybe thirty people there and they erupted at the sight me. They started yelling at me, mostly about what they hoped would happen to me in the near future. One big burly guy who looked like he could've been a bouncer at a club made a charge at me. Two of the other people in the crowd were able to get in his way and pull him back, but he kept trying to break free, red-faced and spittle flying off as he yelled at me. I don't know why he thought I wouldn't have broken his wrist if he had put a hand on me, but I guess the thought hadn't occurred to him.

I stood for a moment trying to pick out their individual voices to see if I could recognize the joker who had been calling me on the cell phone, but there was too much noise coming from them for me to be able to do that. Faces in the crowd did seem familiar, and I realized how much some of them resembled the men that I'd taken out, in particular, the thick-bodied bouncer-type who had gone after me. I tried to remember who he had looked so much like, but couldn't quite pull it out of my memory.

I gave up the effort of trying to match their faces with my past targets, and pushed my way through them so I could get into the courtroom. They followed me in, still shouting at me. The court clerk, a short gnome-like man with a stooped back, looked up, startled by the commotion, and warned them to be quiet or they would be arrested. They didn't stop until the bailiff took a few menacing steps in their direction while shouting for them to shut up. After that they took their seats, but their faces showed their rage.

I took a seat in the front row. The clerk appeared visibly shaken as he looked over the courtroom. After a few minutes the judge entered the room from his chambers. He was tall and thin and with a pink face and a full head of wavy white hair. The clerk had us all rise as he announced him, and the judge took his time walking to the bench. After he was seated, the clerk approached him for a short conversation, and the judge quickly looked annoyed at what he heard. Clearing his throat, he addressed the court as the clerk had earlier, warning that outbursts would not be tolerated.

"I understand that emotions may be running high," he said, his pale blue eyes scanning the room, "but if any of you make a disturbance you will be taken out in handcuffs and arrested. Do I make myself clear?"

He waited until a couple of members of the crowd nodded before he asked the clerk to call out the parties of Dunn vs March.

The wife and two sons of John Dunn were the plaintiffs in the suit. Dunn was one of the men with Douglas Behrle when I shot up the Datsun they were in. Dunn's wife was about my age and looked gray and used up, as if there just wasn't much left of her any more. The two sons were in their late thirties and neither of them seemed like they wanted to be there. My guess was they were being paid to file their suit against me.

The judge looked at me sitting alone at the defendant's table and asked if I had legal representation.

"Your honor, I'm close to indigent. I don't have any funds to hire a lawyer."

Someone in the crowd snickered behind me and commented on how that was a shame. The bailiff took two angry steps forward, and the judge's eyes shot up as he tried to pick out the guilty party. Only after the room had become deathly still again did he turn back to me.

"What do you mean *close to indigent*?" he asked.

"I was released from prison three weeks ago after serving fourteen years," I said. "I have no savings, no bank accounts, and am still getting state assistance, and will continue to for the next five months."

"Do you have any documentation regarding your state assistance?"

"Yes, your honor."

The bailiff walked over to me for one of the papers I had taken out of my stack, and he brought it over to the judge who studied it carefully before asking me whether I had a job.

"Yes, your honor. I'm working as a janitor making eight dollars and twenty-five cents an hour. My rent is five hundred and sixty dollars a month, which doesn't leave me much, if anything, left over."

The judge turned to the plaintiff's lawyer. "What's the point of this action?" he asked. "Do you have any reason to believe that Mr March has assets that the state doesn't know about?"

The lawyer stood up. He had small dark eyes and a piggish and disingenuous mouth, and I could smell Lombard all over him. "Not exactly, your honor," he said. "But we do believe Mr March will be selling the book and movie rights to his atrocities."

The judge accepted that and smiled at me apologetically. "Mr March," he said, "regardless of your financial situation, you should've arranged for legal counsel to represent your interests. This is a civil proceeding, not criminal, and as such the state cannot provide you free legal help."

A voice spoke out from behind me, "Your honor, Daniel Brest from Brest and Callow. If I could confer with Mr March, my firm may be interested in representing him pro bono."

I turned to see a man standing three rows behind me. He was smiling pleasantly, but it didn't quite mask the shrewdness in his eyes. From the way he was dressed he was clearly doing well – I could make out the same style of Cartier watch on his wrist that I had once taken off one of my targets, plus I'd been around enough cheap suits in my time to recognize an expensive number, and his cost some bucks.

The judge asked me if I'd like to take the attorney up on his offer, and I told him I would.

"Fifteen-minute recess then," the judge said.

The plaintiff's lawyer didn't seem happy about this turn of events, nor did he seem surprised, and he kept his mouth shut. Dunn's widow and two sons sat morosely. If anything they appeared disappointed that they had to be there longer than they hoped for. Daniel Brest came swiftly around the aisle to meet me and offer his hand, and then the bailiff led us to a private conference room. Once we were seated I asked him why he wanted to help me.

"I could feed you the standard boilerplate bullshit," he said. "That we believe every party in a courtroom deserves legal representation, blah, blah, blah. The truth is we want the publicity this case will give us. Also, we'd like to represent you if you choose someday to sell the rights to your life story."

"I don't plan on ever doing that."

He took a contract from his briefcase and handed it to me, as well as a pen. "In case you ever change your mind," he said.

The contract was fully made out and gave Brest's firm exclusive rights to act as my agent in a book, movie or any other media deal, in the event that they successfully represented me in any and all wrongful-death lawsuits filed against me.

"What would be considered successful?" I asked.

"That's defined in a subclause on the last page. But basically, if we're able to limit a judgment against you to an aggregate of fifty thousand dollars."

I didn't bother saying the obvious, that a fifty-thousand-dollar judgment against me didn't sound all that successful. I knew what his answer would be – that that amount of money would be peanuts compared to what the rights to my story could bring in. I tried reading the clauses at the end of the contract, but the print was too small for my eyes, and I had to take him at his word. I went back over the section of the contract that spelled out how they would represent me, and tried to figure out if it would preclude my having Sophie as a co-author. From what I could tell, it wouldn't. "Isn't twenty-five percent high?" I asked, referring to the percentage that his firm would collect on any payment I received.

"That would be fair given the situation," he told me, straight-faced, although I guess there was some truth to it. If you're being extorted, twenty-five percent probably would be fair in most situations. "Besides," he added, "it would only come into play if you decided to sell the rights, which you're telling me you won't."

He looked on pleasantly while I signed and initialed the contract where he told me to. After I handed it back to him he asked for all the documents that I had. He read through them quickly and looked up at me, puzzled.

"Their attorney, Harwood, has filed five separate wrongful-death actions against you?"

"Yeah."

"Why wouldn't he join them into a single lawsuit?"

I shrugged. "They're not doing this for money."

Brest gave me an empty smile. "What's their reason then?"

"Harwood's probably acting for the Lombard family," I said. "These lawsuits are being used to keep me in the Boston area, and maybe to be punitive. I'm sure the Lombard family also likes knowing the dates I'm required to be back in Chelsea."

The way Brest's eyes glazed while he continued smiling his empty smile, he clearly didn't put much stock in my explanation for why the different lawsuits hadn't been grouped into a single action. He noticed the way I was rubbing my temples, and with a knowing wink asked if I was having a migraine.

"I don't think so," I said. "More of a constant dull ache."

"You're lucky," he said. "Migraines can be a bitch."

There was a knock on the door, and the bailiff's voice warning us that the fifteen-minute recess was over. Once we were back in the courtroom, Brest joined me at my table and informed the judge that he would be representing me, then requested that the case be dismissed since I had confessed to the police back in 1993 to murdering John Dunn and the three-year statute of limitations had long since expired. The plaintiff's lawyer dryly argued that the contents of my confession had only been released to the public seven months earlier and it wasn't until then that his clients learned I had murdered their respective loving husband and father.

The judge put up a hand to stop any further discussion on the matter. "I want written arguments delivered to me by Friday," he said. He had a brief consultation with the clerk about the court calendar, then announced that the case would be continued a week from Tuesday. "I will make my decision then whether the statute of limitations has been reached. If I determine it hasn't, the trial will start at that time."

That was it for now. I stood up to see the white-hot anger burning in the faces of the thirty or so spectators seated behind me. I don't know what they were expecting from the court that day – condemnation, punishment, blood – but whatever it was they didn't get it, and they were near beside themselves with grief and rage. It was fucking ridiculous. I was just an instrument for Sal Lombard, and whatever retribution they wanted for me should've been directed at Lombard and his family, but I was an easier target. Lombard's family wouldn't lose sleep over putting them all in the ground next to their same loved ones that I'd already taken care of years earlier.

I almost yelled at them all to grow a fucking pair and face Lombard's boys and deal with the ones truly responsible, but

Brest spoke to me first, interrupting my thoughts. I guess he had noticed this mob also.

"Let me show you another way out of here," he said.

I followed him towards the conference room we had gone to earlier, leaving a stunned mob behind us. By the time they realized what was happening we were already out a side door and in a parking lot behind the courthouse. Brest led me to a new BMW sedan, and asked me if he could give me a lift somewhere. I told him South Station, and he said that wouldn't be a problem.

"That looked like it could've gotten ugly back there," he said, referring to the mob we escaped from in the courtroom. "If I can't get the case dismissed, I'll have to try for a change of venue, at least get it out of Suffolk County. Failing that, make sure there's enough police presence so you can get in and out of court safely."

"I wouldn't worry about them," I said. "Deep down they're gutless. Besides, there were others waiting outside the courthouse who were more worth worrying about."

He gave me a curious look, but didn't pursue the subject any further. Instead he told me how he was going to handle the case, that if he couldn't get it dismissed, he'd make the case all about my near destitute situation and how the lawsuits should've been filed against the parties truly responsible, namely the people who had hired me to commit the murders. I only half paid attention to what he was saying. I had more important things on my mind. Like Lombard's two men who were waiting outside the courthouse when I first showed up. They weren't there for their health. I knew I'd be seeing them soon enough. My thoughts also drifted to Sophie. I couldn't help feeling anxious about seeing her later that day.

When Brest pulled up to South Station, he hesitated, then commented on the book and movie rights to my life story.

"It was gold before you put on a cape and tackled those two would-be robbers outside that liquor store, but that just put it over the top." He licked his lips, added, "Leonard, last week I took it upon myself to contact several New York publishing houses. We could get seven figures for a book deal. We just have to put these lawsuits to bed first."

He had earlier given me a business card with his contact information, just as I had given him my cell-phone number and address. As I was getting out of his car, I commented how for twenty-five percent of a seven-figure deal, he should've been giving me taxi service back to my apartment.

"Let's beat these lawsuits first, okay, Leonard?" he said with a half-smile.

I watched him drive off, then walked over to wait for my bus back to Waltham.

Later when I met Sophie she was radiant as she described the scheme she had come up with. "What we'll do is sign a book deal under my name," she told me, beaming from ear to ear. "I'll funnel your share of the money under the table. Fuck any lawsuit filed against you."

It was so damn childish. Any good lawyer would find the money and take it from us. But watching her so happy and proud of herself, I felt a lightness in my heart. She was just so damn beautiful, and in her own way, so damn innocent. I didn't tell her about the contract I had signed with Brest. It didn't matter. If he got rid of the lawsuits without too much damage, I would insist that Sophie be my co-author in any book deal. It would be a tough fight since a publishing house laying out seven figures for a book would want me teamed up with a professional ghostwriter, but I wouldn't back down on the demand, and if they wanted the book bad enough to pay a million plus for it, they'd eventually give in.

I told Sophie we'd do that, that we would write the book together, and then she could try selling it. I figured by the time we had a book completed the lawsuits would be finished with. At least it would give me more time to spend with her in the meantime.

As soon as I agreed to writing the book with her, Sophie put her arms around my neck and kissed me on the mouth. There was no tongue involved, just lips, but there was also no disgust on her face when she pulled away. Only excitement.

"This is going to be so much fun," she said with a throaty purr. "And Leonard, you're not going to regret this, I promise."

I nodded, already regretting this small deception with her, but unable to have done anything else. We agreed on where and when to meet next, and I sat mesmerized watching the swaying of her slender hips as she walked away. I was sitting on a park bench, and my stare stayed fixed on where she had walked off to. Even though she was long out of sight, it was minutes later before I could look away. A young woman pushing a baby carriage reacted with horror on walking past me. She didn't recognize me – that wasn't the reason for her horror. It was something about the way my face had hardened, a transformation that had come over my features while I had been staring after Sophie. After the woman with the baby carriage had nearly run off in a sprint, I got off the bench and headed back to my apartment. It was getting late and I still had a long night of work ahead of me.

When I got back to my apartment building I found a note that had been slipped into my mailbox. It was from Eric Slaine. His paper gave approval for paying me ten grand for an interview, and he wanted me to call him right away.

I took the note to my apartment and carefully read the

contract I had signed with Brest. A week earlier I had bought a pair of magnifying eyeglasses, and used those so I could read all the small print. There was nothing in the contract concerning newspaper interviews.

I didn't want Slaine having my cell-phone number, so I waited until later when I headed off to work and passed a payphone before calling him back. I told him I needed a week to think things over, but I'd call him again. He didn't like it, especially, he claimed, after going to bat for me the way he did. I hung up on him in the middle of his objections.

At work, the same kid was back at the security desk, and like all the other times we didn't say a word to each other when I checked out the keys, later when I checked them back in, or any time in between.

chapter 25

1992

It had been four months since Fred Marzone slipped past me at that Lynn roadside motel. When I later gave Lombard a bullshit story about Marzone already being gone by the time I showed up I thought he was going to put a bullet in my ear himself. Fuck, he was furious. But he calmed down enough to instead poke me several times in the chest with a thick sausage-like finger and warn me that I better not fuck this job up again. That my only priority in life from that moment on was icing Marzone. Since then I've been sent on a dozen wild goose chases, including a week-long trip to Raleigh, North Carolina. It's been getting harder to explain to Jenny why I'm having to take off at the drop of a hat like I've been doing, but I have no choice. Lombard's losing patience, and at this point I don't think he's got much left. If this latest tip turns out as bad as all the others, I might have to change my plans fast and take Lombard out before he tries doing the same to me and my family.

Supposedly Marzone's back in Massachusetts, and this tip has me at a warehouse parking lot in East Boston. It's probably as much bullshit as all the other tips Lombard's been feeding me, but I have to check it out so I am standing by the side of the warehouse shivering in the fucking cold, the wind whipping around and deadening the skin on my face and making the tips of my ears feel like they can be snapped off like icicles. It's one-thirty in the morning, and Marzone's supposed to be here buying a brick of heroin. At least that's the bullshit tip I was given.

I'm about to give up when I see someone lumbering into the parking lot who could be Marzone. He has the same hefty build as Marzone, but he's got his back mostly turned to me so I can't tell for sure. I walk out quietly, my 9mm Luger held at my hip. It's dark, but there's enough moonlight that I'll be able to see his face once he turns around.

When I get within ten feet of him, I yell out, "Hey, Marzone, my buddy, where you been?"

Nine times out of ten that will get them looking behind with a stupid grin plastered on their faces. Marzone, though, takes off like a bat out of hell, faking towards his left then running to his right. My fucking gun jams. I can't believe it. Even with his dumbass juke move I would've separated his spine. I've got another gun on me, a .32 caliber revolver. I start pulling it out of its holster with my left hand, all the while running after Marzone and cursing the sonofabitch every step of the way.

He's gained some ground on me, maybe forty feet in front of me now, and he runs me across streets and through parking lots. I'm panting hard, my chest feeling like it's going to burst, but I keep pushing myself, and Marzone, the dumbass, keeps zigzagging like he's watched too many war movies. The way Marzone's running allows me to make up ground. I'm maybe twenty feet away and am about to take out his right knee with a shot when I hit a patch of ice and my feet fly out from under me. Marzone hears my tumble and stops. When he turns around I can see the indecision in his expression – whether to go after me or keep running. He's panting also, hands on knees, but he's too slow in reacting, too late in making a charge at me, and I'm already scrambling back to my feet. He realizes his lost opportunity, and takes off running again with me following right behind him.

He's running slower now. I'm starting to make up some distance when he does a header on to the pavement, his face taking the brunt of it. A pistol he's been trying to take out of his jacket tumbles out of his hand and clatters harmlessly away. I walk up to him slowly while trying to catch my breath. When I'm standing over him, he looks up at me feebly, his eyes dazed, a good chunk of the skin scraped off his face. I put a bullet in his forehead, then while he's lying dead on the pavement, I put two more in the back of his skull for good measure.

I'm still breathing raggedly, my chest aching, my leg muscles tired and sore. I first slip the worthless piece of shit Luger in its holster, then the .32 caliber. I adjust my pants and jacket and look around quickly. That's when I see her.

chapter 26

present

When I met Sophie on Thursday, she smiled her amused shit-eating grin at me for a good minute or so before I raised an eyebrow and asked her what was up.

"I have a surprise," she said.

"Yeah?"

She pursed her lips as she studied me. Then she told me how she was able to arrange for us to borrow an isolated cabin up in New Hampshire for the weekend.

"From a friend of a friend," she explained. "But we'll be up in the woods and we'll be able to be like real writers. My friend's friend can let us have it from Saturday morning until Monday. That will give us a chance to get started on this book and really concentrate on it."

"I can't do that," I said. "I have to work Saturday night."

She opened her eyes wide in mock surprise. We were sitting at a table in the same coffee shop we had first met in, and the other people there turned to stare as Sophie got out of her chair and walked over to sit on my lap. With her mouth inches from my ear, she said softly, "But Leonard, darling, how can you turn down a weekend alone with a sensual and somewhat attractive younger woman, even though all we're going to be doing there is working."

"Not somewhat attractive," I said. "No, not by a long shot. Let's call you what you are, stunningly beautiful."

She pulled back, grinning at me, her eyes sparkling brightly. "If you say so, Leonard," she said, her tone deprecating. "But seriously, call in sick Saturday. What's the worst that can happen? They fire you? Fuck them if they do that, you'll be making more on this book than they could pay you in a lifetime for cleaning their bathrooms. So come on, what do you say?"

"How are we going to get up there?"

"I'll find us a car," she said.

I found myself nodding, almost involuntarily. "Sure, okay, let's do it," I agreed.

"Outstanding." She played with her index finger lightly along my lips for a few seconds, then kissed me on the cheek. Moving her mouth so she was again whispering in my ear, she said, "I'm not getting you too excited sitting on your lap, am I, Leonard? Because we're only going to be working up there."

"Not enough yet to give me a stroke. But keep trying."

She laughed at that, her head tilted back slightly, the soft curvature of her throat making me swallow hard.

"I guess I can be a bit of a tease," she said. "I'm sorry about that, Leonard, but it's going to be so much fun us working together, and the thought of it has put me in a playful mood." She stopped as she glanced at a clock on the wall. "Shit," she said, her smile fading, "I have to get going, but let's meet right in front of this shop Saturday morning at eight. We'll get an early start."

I nodded, and she hopped off my lap and headed fast towards the door. Before she went through it, she turned to give me a short wave and a slight impish smile.

*

Lombard's boys showed up that night. I was vacuuming one of the third-floor offices when they walked in, the same two who'd been standing outside the courthouse Monday morning watching for me. One of them turned off the vacuum cleaner. The other one told me we were leaving.

"What's the point?" I asked. "If you're going to take me out, just do it here."

He shook his head sadly. "Fuck, I'd like to, but orders are to deliver you alive. Get moving."

I stayed where I was. I was deciding whether I had any chance against them when the one who had turned off the vacuum cleaner took a step towards me, violence in his eyes. "We can rough you up for convincing's sake," he said. "It would be a shame to get blood all over this nice carpeting, but if you need us to do that, sure, why the fuck not."

I told him that wasn't necessary and walked out of the room with them close enough behind for me to feel their breath on my neck and smell the sourness of it. I headed towards the back staircase, figuring they wanted to avoid the lobby and the security desk, but they indicated for me to take the elevator. When we got in there, they crowded me from both sides.

"Will it do me any good asking the security guard for help?" I asked.

"None," the one on my right said. "Except for giving us an excuse to pop you in the mouth."

"This has been the set-up from the beginning," I said. "That's the only reason I was hired here, wasn't it?"

The one crowding me on my left smirked at that but didn't answer me. When we got out at the lobby and they marched me past the security desk, the kid working there looked alarmed. He jumped out of his seat and started yelling, "Hey, hey, hey!"

One of the wiseguys gave him a confused look, and the kid

told him he needed the office keys back. They searched through my pockets, found the keys and tossed them on to the security desk. The kid then picked up his magazine and went back to reading as they took me out the door.

There was a black Cadillac sedan waiting at the curb. I got in the back seat with one of the wiseguys while the other one took the wheel. We drove in silence for a while, and once I realized we were heading back towards Boston I asked them where they were taking me.

"Shut up," the one next to me ordered.

"What's the big deal, why not just tell me?" I asked. "Wait, I got it, this is some sort of surprise party you Revere guys have planned for me and you don't want to ruin it, right? Christ, I'm touched by the sentiment."

The driver snickered, said, "Funny guy you got back there." The wiseguy sitting next to me glared at me for a long moment before warning me again to *shut the fuck up, already.*

I sat back and watched as we sped down the Mass Turnpike. I stayed quiet until we had gotten off of the Turnpike and navigated down several side streets on the way towards Revere.

"This is a hell of a comfortable ride," I remarked. "When I was working for Sal Lombard I had to keep a low profile and was never able to buy myself anything like a Cadillac. Damn nice car, though."

"You like the ride, huh?" the driver said, half under his breath. "That's nice."

"Why'd the two of you wait until now?" I asked. "I've been out almost a month."

"How many times do I have to tell you to shut your mouth?" the wiseguy next to me said. Then, to the driver, he said, "Can you believe this old fuck? He must have Swiss cheese for brains."

The driver got a laugh out of that. I ignored it, said to the wiseguy next to me, "For Chrissakes, you can answer a few questions. I'm going to be dead soon anyway, right?"

"Not soon enough. So just shut your damn ugly piehole already!"

I shook my head sadly at him. "What a couple of fucking embarrassments Lombard's family's hiring these days," I said. "You can at least be civil. Especially since I was about to tell you how you fucked things up."

The last few minutes his face had slowly been reddening. With that comment of mine his color dropped to a harsh icy white. He stared open-mouthed at me for a moment, then pulled a big piece of iron from his shoulder holster and brought it up with the idea of striking me with it. I moved a lot faster than he probably thought I was capable of, blocking his gun hand, and at the same time punching him in the throat with my other fist. He was useless then. Fear flooded what had moments before been dead, hard eyes, and he sat paralyzed, making choking noises.

The driver looked over his shoulder, worried by what he was hearing. "Joey, what the fuck's happening back there?" he asked.

As he tried to see what was going on in the back seat, enough of his face showed from behind the headrest for me to kick him, and I caught him hard enough in the jaw to bounce his head off the driver's-side window. The car crashed into a utility pole seconds after that.

I was still holding on to the other wiseguy's gun. It wasn't hard pulling it out of his hand. He was panicking too much about whether he'd be able to breathe again. I craned my neck forward so I could look over at the front seat. The driver was breathing but out cold.

The wiseguy next to me was still struggling to breathe, his

face having turned a dark purple. All at once he gasped in a frantic breath, then he was back among the living. His eyes were fearful as they turned back to me. He must've remembered stories that he had heard about me. I was no longer just some old cadaverous-looking has-been.

"You've got two choices," I told him. "Either I blow you and your partner's brains out right now, or you answer every question I ask you without hesitation. If you do that I'll leave the two of you alive in the trunk. You've got five seconds to decide."

I slid the safety off a .40 caliber automatic and pushed the muzzle hard into his ear. He winced at that, and told me he'd tell me anything I wanted to know.

"Who are you doing this for?" I asked.

"Nick Lombard."

I was surprised by that. I had never met any of Sal Lombard's sons, but I knew Nick was the youngest, and from what I'd heard, the softest.

"Nick's running things now?"

The wiseguy nodded, his eyes clenched shut.

"Where were you going to take me?"

He was trying hard not to shake but it was a losing battle. "Winthrop. Terrace Avenue," he said.

That brought back memories. They were taking me to the same house where I'd had my initiation all those years ago. I pushed the gun barrel harder into his ear making his grimace tighter.

"Who's waiting for me there?"

"Nick."

"Just him?"

"Yeah."

"One more time, and answer this as if your life depends on it. Because it does. Who's waiting for me in that house?"

"Just Nick, I swear."

He was telling me the truth. He was too scared to be doing anything other than that. I pulled the gun from his ear and had him help me lift the driver into the trunk. There was some rope back there which I had him use to tie up his unconscious companion, then I had him crawl in there also and lie on his stomach while I tied his hands behind his back.

"You know how you fucked up before?" I asked. "You never should've brought me in the back seat with you. You should've put me where you and your buddy are right now."

"You looked too frail for that," he said. "I thought you'd die on us if we did that."

It was a valid point. I closed the trunk on both of them.

The car was dented in front but still drivable. I got in the driver's seat and headed off to Winthrop.

chapter 27

1992

She's bundled up in a heavy green winter parka, but from her shoes and the little I can see of her uniform, I'm guessing she's a nurse. She's young, and her stare keeps moving from Marzone lying dead on the pavement to me standing over him. Her face is so pale in the moonlight. She wants to scream but she's too horrified to do so. I just feel sick inside as I watch her, wishing that there was some other way than what I was going to have to do.

Finally the terror releases her enough to let her move. She starts running, but she has those heels on, and there's ice on the ground, and it's not too long before she falls and lands on one knee. She's crying now. I don't think she has the strength to try running again. My stomach is all knotted up as I walk over to her. I take out the .32 caliber and place the muzzle so it's a few inches from her temple. Her mouth is gaping so wide open that when she cries thick strands of saliva drip from it. Oh Christ. I can't pull the trigger. I just can't do that to her face, not that type of damage. Instead I try hushing her and end up suffocating her, then lower her lifeless body to the ground. At least she looks undisturbed this way. Like she could be sleeping.

For the first time I look around to see where I am, and realize Marzone led me to the back parking lot of a small shopping plaza. There must be a hospital nearby, and this girl was probably cutting through the parking lot as a shortcut home after a late shift. This was all supposed to go down in a desolate warehouse parking lot with the Luger having an attached silencer. Instead I shot off three rounds with a .32, and for all the fuck I know neighbors nearby have already called the police about gunshots. I have to get out of there but I can't leave the girl's body with Marzone. Lombard's furious enough with how this has gone so far and having this nurse's death tied to Marzone would put him over the top.

I jog over to an old rusted Ford station wagon. When I'm on a job like this, I always carry a slim jim and a screwdriver on me. It takes only seconds to unlock the driver's door, and not much longer than that to strip and hotwire the ignition. I drive the car over to the dead nurse and, after popping the trunk, drop her body inside.

The police still haven't shown up, no sirens either, which means I've caught one break tonight. My hands are shaking as I drive away.

I feel so damn cold inside my skull. At first I think about leaving her body someplace where it could be found so her family can have a funeral for her, but I realize how risky that is. I have to make sure her body disappears for good, which isn't hard, but still, I hate the idea of it. I hate the thought of how I'm going to be spending the next few hours.

It takes me an hour to drive where I have to go. The coldness deep in my head has traveled to the pit of my stomach, and it just keeps getting worse. By the time I stop the car, I'm drenched in a sickly cold sweat, and that stench of death nearly overpowers me.

I open the trunk and lift her body from it, except she comes alive in my arms and starts fighting me. Somehow I hadn't killed her the first time, and I feel even sicker inside knowing that I have to do it now for real.

chapter 28

present

The only light inside the house came from the kitchen. I crouched outside one of the windows and watched while a man in his thirties sat alone at a small Formica table, one of his legs tapping anxiously as he chain-smoked his way through half a pack of cigarettes. He had a much skinnier body type than Sal Lombard, but there was enough resemblance in his face – especially that familiar cruel mouth – to know he was Lombard's son. It was possible there were other people inside the house, but I didn't think it was likely. Anyway, it didn't much matter if there were.

I went back to the front door and knocked. I heard footsteps, then the same voice that had been calling me on my cell phone yelling through the door, "Yeah?"

I muffled my voice with my coat, and doing my best to impersonate one of the wiseguys, said, "Fucksake, Nick, it's Joey. We got your merchandise. Open the fucking door."

"You got a death wish talking to me like that?" the man inside yelled back out. There was nothing but mottled fury in his face as the door flung open, then a stunned dumbness as he stood staring at me. Before he could react I tapped him on the forehead with the butt of the gun I was holding, and he sat down hard on the floor. I let myself in and closed the door behind me.

"Hands behind your neck."

He blinked stupidly at me for a few seconds before complying. I patted him down but he wasn't carrying.

His eyes darted left and right before settling on me. He asked, "Where are my men?"

"They're in their car," I said, "and they're not in any position to help you."

"What the fuck do you think you're doing?" he demanded, trying poorly to force a bravado. I raised a finger to silence him.

"It's not going to work that way," I said. "Right now I either kill you, or the two of us figure out a way so I don't have to."

The way his lips twisted, he was about to make a snide comment, but something about my expression made him look away from me instead.

"What do you suggest?" he asked without much hope.

"First some questions. Why'd you wait until now?"

His mouth weakened momentarily. He lowered his gaze. "The FBI was watching you," he said. "They were using you as bait hoping I'd go after you. It was only last week when I found out from my source that they dropped their operation."

I remembered the blue Chevy sedan that Sophie had run up to warn me about. I could almost see the faces of the two men in it. I remembered the other times I'd catch glimpses of other cars waiting for me after work. It made sense that it would've been the Feds watching over me.

"Why wait even a week?" I asked.

He made a face. "I wasn't sure until today I was going to go through with this. I was trying to get past what you did, ratting us out and putting my pop and my brother Al away, but then seeing you being built up like a hero was too much."

"Did your boys search my apartment?"

"I don't know where you live," he said. "If someone searched your place it wasn't us. Probably the Feds."

I considered that for a moment, then asked, "Was the plan tonight to torture and kill me?"

A hitch showed at the side of his mouth. "I was first going to get some information out of you," he said.

"That office building hired me for you?"

He nodded. He was trying hard to keep his composure, but he was cracking. His voice wasn't quite right, and a tic had started to pull at his left eye.

"Why the anonymous calls to my cell phone?" I asked.

He shrugged. "I was trying to let off steam, but it didn't do much good. In the end I had to have you brought here." He hesitated for a few seconds, then asked, "Any ideas yet so you don't have to kill me?"

His skin color wasn't looking too good, neither was that tic pulling on his eye. If I kept him sitting there much longer he was going to expire on me. I had him get up and sit on a loveseat, and I pulled up a wooden chair so I could sit opposite him.

I said, "The only thing I can think of is for you to give me something incriminating enough so you can't afford to let anything happen to me."

He gave it some thought and nodded. "I've got something like that," he said. "It's back at my house."

"You also have to pay me something. A lot actually. How much cash can you get your hands on tonight?"

"Maybe twenty grand," he said.

I whistled softly. "Twenty grand? That's how little you value your life?"

I raised the gun to level it at his chest and his eyes bulged at the sight of it. He told me then that he had over a hundred grand that he could give me. "It's buried right in this basement," he said in a voice that showed fear, but also how disgusted he was with himself. "I keep it there as an emergency fund."

I followed him downstairs and watched as he pulled back a section of the carpeting. He then removed a part of the subflooring that had earlier been cut away and started digging with a shovel. The stress of the situation was getting to him, weakening him, and it wasn't too long before he was sweating and his arms were shaking like they were made of rubber.

"Take a deep breath," I said. "Concentrate on what you're doing. As long as the money's there and you're not lying to me you have nothing to worry about."

"The money's there," he grunted. His breathing remained labored as he struggled to lift each shovelful of dirt. "You should rot in hell," he said angrily, tears mixing with his sweat. "Pop died in prison because of you. After everything he did for you, you gonna betray him like that? He gave you a Rolex, even had it personally inscribed, you rotten sonofabitch!"

"Yeah, he did," I said. "It was a nice one too. And someone in his organization tipped off the Boston Police to what was going down at the docks. So fuck your pop, and fuck your brother Al, too."

Nick's face was locked in a hard grimace. Sweat poured off of him as he shook his head. "The tip didn't come from us, you paranoid fuck," he said. "It came from South Boston."

I thought about what he said and decided it probably made sense, but still, Lombard should've had better control of the operation and not shared it with the South Boston crowd.

"Well, my mistake, then," I said. "But fuck it, no use now crying over spilt milk. And watch your goddamn mouth with me. I'm not warning you again."

He clamped his mouth shut after that and focused on his digging. It was another twenty minutes before he hit a wood plank. He pried it out with the shovel, then reached in and pulled out a valise. Inside were packets of bills wrapped in cellophane.

"You can count it if you'd like," he said. "There's over a hundred grand in there."

"I'll take your word for it. Let's go get your incriminating evidence."

I followed him up the stairs and out of the house. Nick Lombard saw the Cadillac parked off in the distance.

"Let me check on my guys," he said. "I want to see they're okay."

I waved my gun at him, dismissing the idea. "For now they'll keep where they are."

He had a red Mercedes sports coupe convertible parked off to the side. I took the passenger seat while he got behind the wheel. It was a shame it was too cold to put the top down. When we drove past the Cadillac, I could see the worried glance he gave it.

chapter 29

1992

Sal Lombard pours both of us glasses of Dewar's. While I'm sipping my scotch, he takes a couple of Montecristos from a box and offers me one. I decline and he cuts the end off his and lights up. After several puffs, the room's clouding up with the pungent smell of tobacco. I was never one for cigars. Not much for scotch either.

Sal and I are alone, although he's got several of his boys in the room next door. The two of us both went through a lot of trouble to make sure we weren't followed to this hotel suite. It's important that we keep our association hidden from the authorities, which is why we rarely meet face to face. When we do, it's usually at a suite like this one. Lombard has several of them rented anonymously throughout the city, and he takes the necessary precautions to make sure the Feds don't have a clue about them.

"Lenny, what's so fucking urgent?" he asks, his eyes bugging out to show his impatience.

I can't help feeling that he already knows what I'm going to tell him, and I remember the other hit man in his employ that I took out years ago. I know he's not going to let me retire. I know why his boys are sitting in the room next door. Still, Sal's smart enough to know that before they'd get to me I'd have his jugular sliced open.

I drain my scotch and start to tell him how screwed up things went with Marzone.

"Don't worry about it, Lenny," he says. "Marzone was always a slippery fucker, but you finished the job. That's all that matters."

I shake my head. "This job was cursed from the beginning," I say. "When I finally catch up to him my piece of shit Luger jams on me. Then the sonofabitch takes off and runs me a good mile through the streets of East Boston before I catch up with him for the second time. How the fuck I wasn't spotted that night, I still don't know. Sal, I think this was a sign for me to quit this shit."

I sit quietly after that with my hangdog expression. I don't tell him about the girl in the bulky green parka, or what I had to do to her. I don't tell him how young and innocent she looked or how I'm haunted every night now by the memory of what I had to do to dispose of her body. Or how hard it is for me now to close my eyes without seeing her. If I told him any of that I'd be dead. We'd both be dead.

Sal's appraising me quietly. All at once he breaks out laughing. It's a quiet laugh, his body convulsing with it. It's a while before his body stops shaking like jelly. Once that happens, he wipes a few tears from his eye and smiles broadly at me.

"You telling me because of a couple of bad breaks you want to quit?" he says. "I don't believe it, Lenny. I know you, I know what's in your blood. You can't quit this. You'd be fucking miserable."

"It's a sign, Sal—" I try telling him.

"Fuck that. It was a few tough breaks, but you nailed the motherfucker in the end. Right now you're feeling sorry for yourself. You'll snap out of it. Take your wife and kids to Florida for a few weeks. You'll be as good as new when you come back."

I shake my head. "I can't do this any more. I'm sorry."

He grows very quiet, his eyes nearly lifeless as he studies me. Finally, he says, "I can't let you quit, Lenny. I know you're smart enough to know that."

I nod, but don't bother saying anything. We're both staring at each other now. He knows what I'm thinking just as I know what he is. He knows what will happen if he calls out for his boys in the next room.

"Where does this leave us?" he asks softly.

"I don't know."

"Is it only the hits you don't want to do? What about still working for me?"

"It depends. What do you have in mind?"

Sal pours himself a fresh glass of Dewar's. He takes his time drinking it, all the while giving me a hard look.

"I'm starting up a new business by the docks," he says. "It needs a smart guy in charge, which you fucking are even if you're going to give me this bullshit about you not being a killer any more. You still up to some rough stuff if necessary?"

"If necessary."

"Okay then."

He fills up my glass and we drink a toast to our new venture. Whatever moment of danger that had existed between us has passed.

chapter 30

present

Sophie had an ancient-looking Volvo parked outside the coffee shop Saturday morning. I threw an overnight bag into the back seat, then joined her up front. She handed me a large coffee and a muffin that she had bought earlier at the shop, which I gladly took from her. The weather had turned colder – the type of cold where you can see your breath – and I held the coffee with both hands to warm them.

"Thanks for this," I said, acknowledging the food and coffee. I looked hesitantly at the interior of the car, adding, "You sure this tin can can drive? This car has got to be at least thirty years old."

Sophie smiled at that. It was a nice smile. With no makeup on, her thick hair pulled back into a pony tail, and wearing a ratty sweatshirt and a torn pair of jeans, she still looked more gorgeous than most women would look dolled-up and dressed to the nines.

"Not to worry," she said. "My friend promised me it will get us there and back. I also rented us a laptop computer. As long as we can figure out how to use it we'll be playing writer this weekend. Excited?"

"Sure."

She put her hand on my arm and gave me a slight squeeze. "You don't look too excited. Come on, Leonard, cheer up, this is going to be fun. An adventure."

"I am glad we're doing this," I said.

"So am I," she said. She handed me a piece of paper with hand-written directions scrawled on it. "The first few hours we're just going straight up Route 93, then the directions get a little complicated and I'll need your help... Leonard, darling, what's so amusing?"

I waved it off. "Nothing," I said. "Just some random thought."

She gave me a funny look. "Save those for the book," she said. "A little humor won't hurt."

She had a small stack of cassette tapes, and smiled as she told me they came with the car. She asked me what I wanted to listen to and I told her to choose, and she plugged in The Grateful Dead. For most of the trip I sat back deep in thought over what had happened during the past few days and what was going to be happening in the near future, and was barely aware of the music Sophie was playing or the scenery we were passing. Every once in a while I'd look over at Sophie. The excitement burning on her was palpable, and I don't think she had ever looked more beautiful.

After we got off Route 93, the directions did get a little tricky, but we were able to navigate to the cabin, which really was in the middle of nowhere. I ignored Sophie's protests, and loaded myself up with the laptop and all the other baggage and food that she had brought, leaving her to carry only her handbag.

"This is ridiculous, Leonard," she told me. "I'm not some weakling. I can carry some of that."

"I wouldn't think of it," I said, puffing only slightly from my exertion.

After she unlocked the cabin door, I went in first, telling her I'd find the kitchen and put the stuff in there. Instead, though, I put it all down quietly and stood just inside the door so I was behind her when she walked in, taking a canister out of her handbag. She never even knew I was there until I had her arm twisted behind her back and forced the silver canister out of her hand.

"Leonard, please—" she started to say.

The canister had no markings or labels printed on it. I sprayed it in her eyes. A small stream came out of it, and Sophie immediately went into convulsions. I let her drop to the old-fashioned pine-board floor. I could smell immediately that she had emptied her bowels.

Her handbag was one of those large affairs, almost like a small duffel bag. I went through it and found other items of interest. Scalpels, things that looked like dental instruments, and other tools that looked like they could induce great pain. Sure enough I found what I was searching for: a roll of masking tape. Sophie was still going through convulsions when I taped her wrists behind her back and her ankles together. I noticed her nose had started bleeding and a thin stream of blood leaked out of one of her ears. I pulled up a rocking chair and sat and waited until her convulsions stopped. It took a while, but eventually she settled down.

"A nerve agent?" I asked her.

She nodded. "A mild one," she said in a hoarse, weak voice. She was obviously drained from what she had just gone through, and her skin color was awful, but she looked like an entirely different person. She was still beautiful, but there was an iciness about her, almost like she was made from metal. Whatever warmth and vulnerability she had displayed before had been stripped away. I know this must sound funny since she was probably never more vulnerable in her life, but what I saw lying there was more machine-like than human. Beautiful, even still.

"Does it have any long-term side effects?"

"I don't know."

"Was there ever any attraction between us?" I asked.

"None. I never found you anything but repulsive. It was all an act."

She didn't say this to be mean or hurtful, nothing more really than giving me the facts. Besides, she wasn't telling me anything that I hadn't known all along, at least on some deep subconscious level.

"Let me guess, you were never sexually abused as a child, nor did you ever serve time in prison," I said.

"I had a happy childhood. And no, I never did time."

"You put on a damned good act," I said.

"Thanks, but obviously not good enough. What gave me away?"

I shrugged. "I never told you I was working as a janitor, yet you made a comment about me cleaning toilets for a living."

Her eyes dulled as she digested that. Of course I could've told her I'd researched her name at the library and all I could find was an obituary for a girl in Minnesota who had been killed three years earlier in a hit-and-run. I could have also told her how at some gut level I knew the instant I saw her what she was. I might've been in denial about it, but I must've known then. I saw no reason to make her feel any worse than she did so I didn't tell her any of that.

"Why'd you go through this whole elaborate set-up?" I asked her. "You had so many opportunities to kill me before this."

"I'm not sure that's true," she said. "I had researched you enough to know how difficult it would've been if I didn't gain your trust first. Even if I were camped out on a rooftop with a high-powered rifle, from what I know about you, you probably would've sensed it. Besides, I wasn't hired just to kill you. My job was more complicated than that."

"What were you hired for?"

"To find out what you did to my client's sister. Then to make you suffer pretty badly before killing you."

"What do you mean *client's sister*?"

She winced as blood from her ear dripped into her eye. "Does the name Sally Hughes ring a bell?"

I thought back on the girl in the bulky green parka. Back then I didn't want to know her name, so I never looked inside her pocketbook. "No," I said.

"It should. You murdered her in 1992 and made sure her body was never found."

"I never killed a woman before," I said.

She smiled weakly at that. "Leonard, I'm being straightforward with everything I'm telling you, you can show me the same professional courtesy. Seven months ago, when my client found out that you had murdered Fred Marzone, she knew that you had murdered her sister also. Sally was working at a hospital nearby where you had left Marzone's body. Judging from where she lived, she would've been cutting through that same parking lot if she was walking home after work."

She broke into a coughing fit. It didn't sound too good, and after it stopped, she smiled weakly at me again. "My client tried to get the police to reopen their investigation into Sally's disappearance, but they refused to. Their reason was that you would've added Sally's murder to your confession if you had actually done it. Leonard, I've been curious about this. Why didn't you admit to killing her? With the deal you had worked out there would've been no consequences for it."

"I didn't kill her," I said.

Sophie's eyes went blank. "Okay," she said, flatly.

"A few weeks ago you searched my apartment, didn't you?"

"Yes, I did. I was looking for any trophies you might've taken off of Sally. I didn't find any. I did find the money you taped inside your radiator, but I left that alone. I also saw all your little matchsticks and other safeguards, but I figured you would come to the conclusion that Lombard searched your place, so I didn't bother replacing any of it."

"Is the sister coming here?"

Sophie hesitated for only a second before nodding. "She'll be here in an hour," she said. "She wanted to watch while I inflicted pain."

"My own curiosity – how much is she paying you?"

"A lot."

"How much is a lot?"

She gave me another weak smile. "A quarter of a million dollars. Leonard, I'd like to make another request for professional courtesy. I've soiled myself and I'm bleeding from my ear and nose and I'm nauseous like you wouldn't believe. Can you make this quick, and end this already?"

"Sophie, I don't want to kill you," I told her. "I want to somehow get through this without having to do that. What I'm going to do is move you to one of the bedrooms, then wait for your client to show up. I didn't kill her sister, and I'll find a way to convince her of that, and…"

And fuck it.

There are only so many lies you can stack on top of each other before they come tumbling down on you. Early on most of the lies were to myself. Deep, deep denial, you know. As much as I tried convincing myself otherwise, I knew on some subconscious level why I had to stay in the Boston area after I was released from prison. I had to be there for Lombard and his boys to make a play for me. And if not them, then someone else holding a grudge.

You see, I'm not a madman. I'm not some psychopathic killer who can just grab their victims at random. I don't get sadistic pleasure from my killings, and I certainly don't enjoy seeing my victims suffer. But I do need to kill. It's something ingrained deep in my core. Until recently I've been trying to pretend that wasn't so; I wanted badly to hold on to this idea of me being a different person, but I can't do that any more. That's okay. I can deal with what I really am as long as the killings are the result of a job or my acting in self-defense. As long as I'm not just some crazy lunatic running around slaughtering people.

For years I tried to convince myself that I was only doing a job for Lombard, that I could've just as easily ended up a bartender or a construction worker, or working any other nine-to-five job. I tried to hide from the knowledge of what was really inside me, and I think all of that denial and self-delusion was what caused my headaches. Even though I didn't understand it at the time, the need to kill again was the real reason I defended Lucinda inside her diner – I must've been hoping that that dirtbag would be waiting outside for me and would give me my excuse. It was the same reason I must've also broken up that robbery outside the liquor store. Yeah, those punks attacked me, but they were so feeble at it that I wouldn't have been able to justify self-defense if I had killed them. Maybe to a court, but not to myself. And I guess that was the same reason I let myself get hooked up with Sophie and build this idyllic fantasy about her.

And now for the lies that I haven't just been telling myself. The way I had already described it with the two wiseguys was mostly true. But after I had them in the trunk, I didn't tie them up. I shot them both in the head. And Nick Lombard? After he dug up the money for me, I put two bullets in his chest and left him dead in the cellar. Anything else would've been insane.

And Sophie...

She's in another room now, but that's only so I don't have to smell her. I ended it for her right after she asked me to. And I made it quick.

Now I'm sitting here waiting for Sophie's client. Sally Hughes's sister. When she gets here I'll be killing her too, but I'll make it fast. She'll be gone before she even knows what happened. I know what some of you are probably thinking, that the decent thing would be for me to tell her about Sally, but I don't see it that way. It wasn't pleasant how I disposed of the body, and I don't see why I should burden her with that knowledge. Why ruin her last few moments like that? Better for her to hold on to the thought that she's entering the house to see me tortured.

It turns out there was over a hundred and twenty thousand in the valise that Nick Lombard dug up for me. After all my lawsuits are finished with I'll use that money to change my identity and set up shop where I can continue my profession. Fuck any book deals and fuck any interviews. Eventually I'll slip back into anonymity. I might look a little familiar to my clients, but not enough where they won't hire me.

I realize I'm content. My headaches are gone and have been ever since Thursday, and I know they're not coming back. It's a relief when you finally admit to yourself what you are, and in my case, that I'm a killer. I wish I had told Sophie what I found so funny earlier when she explained the route to the cabin, since she's one of the few people who could've appreciated the humor – that she was trying to have me give directions to my own execution. In a way it was a shame I had to do to her what I did – we could've made a good team. Even if she did find me repulsive.

As I sit back I can smell the scent of death saturating my skin. That's fine, it doesn't bother me any more, and nobody else has ever seemed to notice it.

I hear a car pull up and I brace myself. Once I hear the footsteps on the gravel outside, I move over to the doorway and hide in the shadows of the room.

I understand how hard it must've been for her over the years, not knowing what had happened to her sister, and how torn up she must've been after convincing herself that I was the person responsible. Since she had hired a professional to kill me, I can justify now killing her as self-defense, but I can still appreciate the cruelty of it, and I almost feel sorry for her. Almost.

The door opens.